TRINITY JESSICA LOUISE

Mazi Mcburnie

Author's Tranquility Press
ATLANTA, GEORGIA

Copyright © 2024 by Mazi Mcburnie

All rights reserved. No part of this publication may be reproduced, distributed or transmitted in any form or by any means, including photocopying, recording, or other electronic or mechanical methods, without the prior written permission of the publisher, except in the case of brief quotations embodied in critical reviews and certain other noncommercial uses permitted by copyright law. For permission requests, write to the publisher, addressed "Attention: Permissions Coordinator," at the address below.

Mazi Mcburnie /Author's Tranquility Press
3900 N Commerce Dr. Suite 300 #1255
Atlanta, GA 30344, USA
www.authorstranquilitypress.com

Ordering Information:
Quantity sales. Special discounts are available on quantity purchases by corporations, associations, and others. For details, contact the "Special Sales Department" at the address above.

Trinity Jessica Louise / Mazi Mcburnie
Paperback: 978-1-964362-81-6
eBook: 978-1-964037-80-6

Contents

DEDICATION ....
Chapter 1 1
Chapter 2 9
Chapter 3 15
Chapter 4 24
Chapter 5 30
Chapter 6 36
Chapter 7 49
Chapter 8 51
Chapter 9 57
Chapter 10 65
Chapter 11 71
Chapter 12 74
Chapter 13 82
Chapter 14 84
Chapter 15 90
Chapter 16 96
Chapter 17 100
Chapter 18 109
Chapter 19 113
Chapter 20 116
Chapter 21 122
Chapter 22 125

Chapter 23	130
Chapter 24	133
Chapter 25	139
Chapter 26	142
Chapter 27	145
Chapter 28	148
Chapter 29	151
Chapter 30	152
Chapter 31	156
Chapter 32	159
Chapter 33	163
Chapter 34	166
Chapter 35	169
Chapter 36	171
EPILOGUE	176

DEDICATION

FOR LYN

AND MY SOUL FOOD SISTERS

Chapter 1

So much loved, so much wanted, so incredibly beautiful, skin pale pink, golden curls, deep enchanting blue grey eyes and a gentle sweet nature. The child was the image of her gorgeous mother, April Langley.

April gazed down at the softly sleeping infant. Her tiny hands were tucked under her soft little blue rabbit. Was it only nine months ago when this tiny miracle appeared, all wrinkled and red, into the waiting arms of her handsome father, ready to cut the cord, as the tears fell gently onto his much-wanted newborn daughter.

Thomas Langley was a rugged looking, strong, tanned farmer, having lived all of his life in the beautiful country homestead where he himself had been born, just on 30 years ago. Nothing prepared him for the enormous rush of love he felt when he saw her for the first time. It was love at first sight. Everything he learnt so far and read about parenthood was true and even more wonderful than he ever could have imagined. His reading of "Bringing up Baby" by Stephanie Myfield spoke about the love which comes from the birth of a child, did not prepare him for the incredible joy which comes with a new baby.

April and Thomas were married for five years now, since university days when they fell in love after meeting in the campus library. They quite literally bumped into each other, laughing together as the books they were holding fell to the floor, and they bent to retrieve them, both at the same time. Afterwards there were many more happy days in the library, and everywhere else, days filled with laughter and love.

At 22 years old, April was a stunning looking natural blonde, with eyes sometimes blue, sometimes grey, a small slim figure with a charming wide smile and infectious laugh. It was love at first sight for Thomas and April, who experienced a rush of love which they had never felt before. Before long, April and Thomas were a couple and madly in love. They did everything together and especially enjoyed their visits to concerts and musicals which happened to be playing at the time in Sydney theatres.

Thomas was studying accountancy, so he could manage the family farm more efficiently, and April was studying for an arts degree, with a view towards teaching. She planned to teach music if the local high school at Springfield offered it to their students. April was an only child, who lost her parents when she was just eighteen in a car accident. She was brought up in the country where her father practiced law in a small country town and her mother taught at the local primary school. Her parents' deaths not long before she met Thomas left her

depressed and upset. There was an aunt living in the north of Queensland, but aside from Aunt Jenny she was pretty much on her own. She usually managed to visit her aunt once a year. April was very lonely until she met Thomas, having no siblings or any cousins to support her.

Thomas came from a large country property in mid NSW. The property was predominately mixed farming. They sowed wheat and corn each year and grew sheep and cattle for the market. Thomas was to take over the farm when his parents retired to live in the small country town near where they lived.

April and Thomas were both twenty-two when they married and moved to Langley Park just outside of the town of Springfield to live, when his parents left for their new home in town. They were married in the little timber church nearby, where Thomas had been baptized years before. Their wedding was delightful, and the reception afterwards which was organized by Thomas's parents was held at the property, Langley Park. There were over one hundred and fifty guests. The Langleys were a popular family who farmed in the area for generations. April wore her mother's wedding gown with a long lace veil and carried a posy of roses in shades of pink from the gardens at Langley Park.

April took to farming like a duck to water, helping out at hectic times such as shearing and lambing or harvest time. She even worked as shearers' cook when it was shearing time. She worked part-time at the local High School teaching music, which was a passion of hers. She thoroughly enjoyed working with her promising senior students. Thomas purchased a grand piano for her use, and she was also accomplished on the violin and the harp. Many evenings were spent around the piano with friends, in summer following a barbeque, or in winter seated around a huge red gum log burning open fire. Somehow the evenings always led to a singalong. April was in constant demand to play the piano at local functions and the organ at church.

April felt blessed to have wonderful in-laws. Thomas's parents were supportive and friendly to her from the first moment she met them. In a way they became her parents.

Their lives were busy and full to the brim with activities and daily chores, and they enjoyed being with many friends of similar ages. April kept chooks, and there were goats and pigs to be looked after, as well as baby lambs during the lambing season. There was always something happening on the property. When she did have any spare time, April enjoyed her vegetable garden, growing all sorts of seasonal vegetables and herbs, or the rose garden, which bordered the entrance leading into the property.

Whilst their busy lives provided fulfillment in many ways, the young couple knew that something was missing from their lives. Both April and Thomas longed for a child to complete their relationship, but in five years of marriage, in spite of numerous tests and visits to specialists, there had been no sign of a pregnancy as the months and then years passed by. Many of their friends

already had babies, making it even harder for April and Thomas. The doctors told them there was absolutely nothing wrong with either of them. They just needed to be patient, and to relax. April was finding it difficult to be patient as time went on.

Sixteen months before, April was feeling under the weather and was very tired. Thomas was concerned and firmly insisted she take a week off school to rest, after a very busy shearing season when she was cooking for the shearers. Coming up with three meals a day, plus morning and afternoon teas for the shearers, was a huge task for one person. At the end of the week off, she was still tired and was feeling a bit nauseous at times, so he insisted she go to town to visit old Dr. Stanley, who was the family doctor for many years. "You are really fussing over nothing Thomas," she said with a smile.

The nurse at the doctor's rooms asked her to put on a gown, and then when Dr. Stanley was ready, she was called into his room. "Hello April. We have not seen you in here for ages," he said. "Well, Dr. Stanley, I really don't think that there is anything wrong with me, but Thomas has been fussing about me and wanted me to come," she answered. "Well let's check you over then," he said with a smile. April hopped onto the examination table, almost certain there was nothing to worry about. She was normally a very healthy young woman.

Leaving the doctor's surgery, April drove the few short kilometers home slowly, trying to digest what Dr. Stanley told her. She did not know whether to laugh or cry. Her emotions were all over the place as no doubt were her hormones.

April arrived home, walking straight through to the kitchen, to find Thomas was putting a roast of lamb in the oven and was preparing potatoes and pumpkin to put in the pan. Smelling the roast all of a sudden, she felt hungry for the first time in a while. He even made mint sauce to go with the lamb.

"How did you go" he asked gently. "Oh, you mean at the doctor's," she replied with a smile. "Well guess what, in about six or seven months, you, Thomas, will become a father. What do you think about being a daddy at last," she asked.

"Yes," shrieked Thomas as he dropped the vegetable peeler and ran to his lovely wife, kissing and hugging her tightly. They both started talking at the same time. It was a moment of pure joy which they would always remember. "When are you due. Are you well?" Thomas bombarded her with questions. "I thought this day would never come," she said happily. "I did not ever give up hope," replied Thomas, with a huge grin on his face.

After months and years of praying and waiting, their dream of becoming parents was about to become a reality.

As the months turned to weeks, preparations for the new arrival went into overdrive, while each of them waited for the big day. Thomas became more watchful as the days were ticked off the calendar. He was very caring, always making sure that April was getting enough

rest, and not overdoing things which she had a tendency to do.

April positively bloomed in her pregnancy, once the first few weeks of initial fatigue and mild nausea passed. She and Thomas started to attend birthing classes in readiness for the big day. She wanted Thomas to be present at the birth and he was just as keen.

Meanwhile, April busied herself making baby clothes on her sewing machine and knitting far too many matinee jackets in colours of white and yellow. April took long walks to keep herself fit for the birth and ate lots of vegetables and fruit. She was very well in her pregnancy, once the morning sickness abated. "

What on earth are you going to do with all of these baby clothes?" asked Thomas with a grin. "Well, I can always donate them to the Red Cross, I suppose," she replied laughing "Or we could have another baby," she added. "One at a time, I think," said Thomas with a grin. "Maybe I will have twins," declared April with a shy smile.

Now, looking back, April could hardly believe they experienced any life at all before she arrived. How could such a small child bring so much love and joy into their marriage she wondered, as she watched her sleeping daughter, hoping that she would wake up soon, so she could have another cuddle. While April knew Trinity needed her rest, she still loved the times when she was awake, so she or Thomas could play with her. She was at an exciting age and loved to play with her blocks and listen to stories read to her by her mother or father.

The day of the baptism arrived, sunny and warm with a faint breeze.

"Name this child," said old Reverend Lycett, at the baptismal font in the little wooden church where Thomas himself was baptized years ago. It was also the same church in which April and Thomas were married, years before.

Thomas and April stood proudly beside the minister with the Godparents looking on. Their little girl was just four months old and was dressed in her father's white Christening gown and shawl, her blue grey eyes sparkling and her tiny hands clutching a silver rattle, a present from Grandma Langley.

"Trinity Jessica Louise" replied April softly as their family and friends watched on.

Chapter 2

It was the one time of the year again. The Springfield Rodeo was ready to begin.

The annual rodeo was a huge event in the small town of Springfield, not far from where the Langley's lived. It was held at the local football stadium. This year it was particularly important to the town because it was the 50th anniversary of the Springfield Rodeo. Every year, hundreds of tourists as well as just about everyone in town, turned up to the two-day event, their utes and four-wheel drives creating small dust bowls around the town as they drove to the stadium, where stalls of food and entertainment to suit the needs of all ages, were ready and waiting to serve the eager visitors. The rodeo was also significant to the district, because of the money which the tourists injected into Springfield.

This year the rodeo was featuring roughriding, saddle bronc and bareback riding and steer and bull riding. Also featuring were timed rodeo events, barrel races and rope and tie, with many other events for enjoyment by young and old.

Thomas and April missed the event last year, due to April's advanced stage of pregnancy and were looking forward to attending this year, along with their new very special family member, Trinity Jessica Louise.

The first few months of caring for their little daughter, Trinity, gave them much joy. She was such a good baby and not an ounce of trouble. April took leave from her teaching to become a full-time mother for her daughter. April breast fed her for six months, and now she was having solid foods and drinking out of a cup. She started to crawl just the week before and April felt she would walk and talk early. Trinity was starting to make sounds like mama and dada. She just turned nine months old a few days ago.

On the day of the rodeo, they packed up a well-worn picnic basket filled with chicken sandwiches, sultana scones and bottles of soft drink in a cooler, as well as baby food for their child, loading it all into their four-wheel drive, already fitted with a baby car seat and sleeping basket.

They left early to get a parking spot close to the oval, joining the queues at the entrance gates along with others, all kinds of people, young and old, some of whom travelled long distances to get there.

They picked a parking spot close to a large gum tree for shade, and also close to a row of seats where they could sit. Their little girl fell asleep in her car seat during the ride in the car from their home. She was teething, and awake a few times during the night before. April brought out cushions and rugs to sit on whilst Thomas carried the food and drinks from the car.

"Shall we leave her asleep for a while?" asked April. "Yes, she went through a rough night, so she needs her rest," replied Thomas. "Besides we will just be a few feet away, sitting on the seats provided for spectators," he added, confident they were close enough to their little girl in order to observe her.

They did not lock their car, leaving the side windows down a bit for fresh air. No-one locked their cars in Springfield.

The rodeo was already starting, with events drawing loud shouting and clapping from the crowds, as sturdy looking men and women completed their turns. Beautifully groomed horses were among the attractions. Small boys and girls ran around with cowboy hats on their heads. Children flocked to the brightly coloured carousels. Thomas and April soon became immersed in the cheering environment but were always aware of their daughter sleeping close by.

Seven minutes later Thomas said, "time to check on our little girl to see if she is awake yet." April stood up and followed him to the car, looking forward to cuddling her little girl.

Amid background noise, they walked the few steps to the car, peeping into the back seat where their daughter slept. There was not a soul in sight as they opened the car door, standing silently, looking at the now empty car seat, where their daughter Trinity was sleeping just seven minutes before.

"No, oh no," screamed April as she realised her beloved daughter was not there, while Thomas began to look around the car, both inside and out. He quickly looked around the area but could not see a soul. "Where is our daughter?" April screamed. April made a dash towards the medical tent where two policemen were stationed. "Help, please help," she shouted, crying hysterically. The older policeman attempted to calm the crying woman in order to find out what was going on. Thomas yelled "Our daughter is missing, she is gone, gone, vanished," he stammered. Finally, the policemen understood there appeared to be a missing child. He immediately put out a call for extra police to attend the scene.

Before long, a search was organised by the police, with volunteers immediately stepping up to help look for the infant. Townspeople and visitors alike joined a massive search of the entire stadium, including cars and seating areas. They searched in the midst of crowds and dust, always present at all rodeos. Searching for anything or anyone at a rodeo was not the easiest task for the police. Two hours later there was still no sign of the little girl. No-one heard or saw anything at all. It was amazing no-one even heard the sound of a baby crying.

The police started a search of the thick bushland surrounding the town in the hope of finding some clues. There were dense redgum forests in the area. Volunteers came from everywhere to search those areas which were usually only seen by bushwalkers or hikers. There was no sign of a baby or any baby items which the searchers could find in their first search.

Trinity Jessica Louise

The day drifted into evening and then to the dark of night. Thomas and April began to feel that their much-adored little girl, Trinity, was missing and most probably was taken by person or persons as yet unknown. Why or how would anyone steal a small child from a car in broad daylight, they wondered. Surely someone must have seen something. A baby could not simply disappear into thin air. How was it possible? Friends helped with the search and surrounded April and Thomas with love and support. Thomas's parents were alerted, and his mother cried her heart out. His father joined in the search for his only granddaughter.

Unfortunately, one of the problems relating to a missing child is the enormous publicity which comes with the abduction, thus hampering the efforts of searchers and police.

Newspaper reporters, as well as television reporters flocked to the property, once the news leaked to the press, hoping to get an inside view or scoop about the missing child. Before nightfall the entire town of Springfield and beyond knew about the missing baby. April and Thomas immediately offered a large reward to anyone who could give information about the kidnapping.

The offer of a reward only added to the nightmare, as people came out of the woodwork to report their fake findings over the next few days and weeks. Someone saw her pink blanket, someone else saw a woman carrying a baby from the rodeo. Another person heard a baby crying next door in a house where old people lived. Another person handed in a rattle. In fact, they received several rattles in many different shades. It went on and on for days. All of the tips were thoroughly checked by the police. but proved to be of no use. This added to the distress felt by April and Thomas.

Chapter 3

"How much fuel have we got Billy, in this crappy car?" asked his mate Jimmy Willis from the back seat of the old Holden car, where he was sitting with his latest girlfriend, Jenny Evans. Jimmy was quite handsome, and many girls chased him, mostly fourteen or fifteen-year-old teenagers. He chose Jenny as his latest girlfriend, because she always seemed to have plenty of money to spend. "Enough to have some fun," shouted Billy Jones. Seated beside him was Mavis Beatty, a large girl of about 16 years old. She was a pretty girl or could be if she took better care of herself. She dyed her hair from mousy brown to blonde, not making a very good job of it. The bottle said it would be breathtaking, it was the opposite in fact, making her look almost like a clown. Giant fake gold earrings hung from her ears and a nose ring decorated her chubby face. Her blouse and jeans were far too tight and made her look bigger than she was. Her tummy was protruding out from the top of her jeans. She looked like a girl whose normal size should be a twenty, squeezed into a size twelve.

Mavis lived with her father old Don Beatty, known throughout Springfield as the biggest boozer in town. He used to work at the local council but lost his job years ago, when he ran over his boss's foot with a tractor while drunk on the job. His boss could never walk properly again. He used the money from the kids' endowment payments to buy grog and cigarettes whilst the three children lived on takeaway fish and chips, or meals at friends' homes. Mavis had an older brother, Kenny and a younger sister, Beverley who had just started high school. Mavis and Beverley were not close. They had totally different personalities. Beverley loved to read and enjoyed school, whereas Mavis hated school and only read comic books.

Don did not consider his children a priority, in fact he considered all three of them to be nuisances. Don's wife had run out on them years ago, when his drinking was at its worst. They never heard from her again and did not have any idea where she lived. Their home was nothing more than a simple shack and two of the children rarely, if at all, attended school. Their clothes were always torn, dirty, or both.

Mavis quit school when she was fifteen, having fantasies of becoming a hairdresser. Since there did not seem to be anyone looking for trainee hairdressers in the small town, Mavis was still unemployed, and most likely unemployable. Mavis did not really want to work. She was more interested in painting her face with garish red lipstick and the latest liquid foundation, advertised on the television "to change your skin from rough to silky smooth overnight". Mavis was very vain.

Billy Jones didn't like Mavis much, but he knew her older brother Kenny and she always seemed to be hanging around, so he put up with her reluctantly. Mavis was a depressing person to be around. Billy himself had a better home life. His father Ted Jones, worked on the railways, and his mother suffered from depression, spending most of her days in bed, so Billy hardly ever went home. "Can't stand my moaning old girl. She never shuts up," he told his mates. At least his father provided food for the table and purchased groceries on a regular basis. His dad did most of the cooking in the home. It was simple fare, but he did his best. They ate mutton chops and mashed potatoes nearly every night. Just occasionally they enjoyed beef mince pies from the local baker.

Jimmy and Billy were mates from primary school, when they attended, which was not often. High school was even worse. They both hated school, never did any homework and were not in the least bit interested in learning. They used to sneak away to the river to go fishing whenever they could and were known to the local police now as troublemakers. Whenever there was a broken window or robbery in town the police always went to Jimmy or Billy first. They were in the Childrens' Court a few times, but due to their ages, always managed to get away with community service.

Jimmy was the youngest of eight children born to Jim and Heather Willis in as many years. After bearing eight children, Heather was sick and tired of children, so spent her days in the world of make believe, watching soap operas on television, while eating boiled lollies and chocolates, sitting on the old, tired couch. The father of the children ran off with Heather's sister Mary, after having an affair with her for years. The three older boys brought money into the house, but Jimmy, being just fifteen was allowed to run wild. His mother never knew what mischief he was getting up to but didn't care anyway. As long as he stayed out of her hair, she was happy, not that she was happy very often. It never bothered her, when the police came calling to discuss something Jimmy had done. She just shrugged her shoulders and told them she knew nothing.

Jenny Evans was an older girl at seventeen, however was not very bright. She was a plain girl with not much to offer in the way of looks. Her hair was straight and mouse brown. Her eyes were green, and she was very flat chested, meaning she never needed to wear a bra. She did nothing to enhance her beauty. She did not have much personality and was a follower rather than a leader.

Her home life was good, her father and mother ran a small hardware business which they both worked in. Jenny was an only child. Her parents were church going and attended bible classes twice each week. They were very strict at home with lots of rules. Jenny rebelled against her religious upbringing, liking the idea of being the girlfriend of the notorious Jimmy Willis. Her girlfriends thought she was lucky to have a handsome boyfriend like Jimmy. She loved to boast about him and how wonderful he was. Jenny followed Jimmy around like a pet puppy and would do anything he asked of her. Jenny's parents were totally unaware she was running around with Jimmy Willis and Billy Jones.

Trinity Jessica Louise

The four young teenagers spent a lot of time together, always on the lookout for mischief of some kind or another. Most of their mischief involved stealing from houses or cars. In country towns, people rarely worried about safety of cars or houses. They thought nothing of stealing cars when they wanted to, especially on a Saturday night when there was not much happening in town except local parties to which the four of them were never invited, or screenings at the local picture theatre. There were however plenty of opportunities for them to steal cars, since no-one bothered to lock them or their houses, in the country town of Springfield.

On the day of the rodeo, they decided not to attend, because they did not have much ready cash to spend, and knowing the police were out in force to catch thieves, making it hard for them to steal anything. Extra police were brought in from other districts to help with the rodeo. "Better not get too close to the rodeo with so many cops around," said Billy. Nevertheless, they hung around the gates of the rodeo grounds, hoping to grab a car. Jimmy spotted a car outside of the rodeo grounds. It was not locked, and the keys were sitting on the front seat. "Hey guys, this one looks good," he said to his mates. "Yep, should do for a bit of fun," replied Billy. "Let's go guys," he said, looking around to see if there were any police nearby.

It was an older model Holden sedan but there was plenty of room for the four of them. Billy hopped into the driver's seat as they commenced doing a few burn outs on vacant crown land, just out of town. "I'm hungry," announced Jenny. "Let's go to the rodeo quickly just to get some food. I have some money," she said. "Yeah, I am hungry too," said Jimmy.

They all agreed, so Billy turned the car towards the rodeo grounds. They grabbed some hot chips at one of the stalls and sat down on the grass under a big gum tree to eat them. Mavis turned around and noticed a car with the windows down a bit. She went to the car and looked in the back seat.

"Gosh, it's a baby," she said in amazement. "Oh, what wonderful luck, "she exclaimed. She opened the car door and gazed at the beautiful baby in the car seat, just waking up with a huge smile on her pretty face. Without thinking too much, Mavis leaned into the car, undid the straps around the car seat and quickly took the baby out of the car, saying to her friends, "Look what I have found, and she is mine, all mine". "You lot can't have her."

Billy jumped up and said, "What the hell, Mavis. What on earth have you done now, you stupid cow?"

Jenny and Jimmy stood in awe as Mavis cuddled the little girl. "I have always wanted a baby, and now I have one. Look at her, she looks just like me with her blonde curls and blue eyes," she said softly. The other three teens thought that Mavis was delusional if she saw any resemblance to herself in the child.

Jimmy said quickly, "Get in the bloody car, Mavis, while we decide what to do about the kid, and before we get caught, you stupid twit. You could get us into a heap of trouble this time."

The four of them got into the stolen car and Jimmy put his foot down on the accelerator, taking off like a madman. Mavis was still holding the baby wrapped in a lovely pink knitted shawl.

Terrified they would get caught by the police for the stolen car and now with a stolen baby as well, the four teens took off, away from Springfield as fast as they could. They decided to go to the next town, about 40 kilometres away, and on the way found some great spots to do burn outs. Fortunately, the car was full of fuel.

It was late afternoon when they stopped outside the next town, got out of the car and lit a small bonfire with some twigs from an old tree, to cook some sausages which Jenny bought at a convenience shop, more like a service station, on the edge of town. Mavis continued to hold the baby, all the time making cooing noises to her. "My baby, my baby, you are so beautiful," said Mavis, with tears in her eyes. "I am going to call my baby Juliet, like in Romeo and Juliet, "she announced proudly.

"Well Mavis, what are you going to do about the kid?" asked Jimmy. "She needs food," said Jenny "Give her a sausage," said Billy. They fed her a sausage and gave her a drink of water. Surprisingly the baby ate the sausage. "She is mine, I want to keep her. I am so lonely. You can't take her from me," replied Mavis. "No bloody way can you keep a kid, you moron," announced Jimmy. "You can't even look after yourself. We will just have to dump her somewhere." "No, no please don't," said Mavis.

"Do you mean like a church or hospital?" asked Jenny. "No way. The cops might find us," replied Jimmy. "Jenny, this is serious trouble if we get caught. Don't you get it?" he added.

Just then the baby started to grizzle a bit. Billy looked around and saw lights in the distance. "Over there," he yelled. It looked like a small farmhouse on the edge of town. "This place will do," said Jimmy. Mavis started to cry as Billy wrenched the child from her and quickly ran to the farmhouse. Mavis tried to stop Billy, but he was too strong for her, even though she was bigger than him. There was a wide outside veranda attached to the house, where he quietly put the baby on a mat at the front door. He threw the blue soft rabbit and the silver rattle down as well. The baby was still wrapped in her pink blanket. He then took off and jumped into the car as fast as he could. The baby started whimpering softly.

Mavis wailed "My baby, my baby. You pigs can't take my baby," as the boys told her to shut up and drove away from the area as fast as they could, dumping the car on the other side of Springfield so the police would not connect the kidnapped baby with the stolen car. The car ran out of fuel anyway. They then walked back into town as if nothing ever happened, going home to their respective houses and sneaking in through open windows, as they normally did whenever they were out making mischief or stealing from the local people of Springfield. With all of the police around they were extremely lucky to not get caught.

Over the next few days and weeks, the four teens became fully aware of the missing child. How could they not, when the entire town was out looking for her. They met in secret late one afternoon, about a week later. They were trying not to be seen together in case the police were watching. They used a favourite meeting place near an old gold mine at the edge of town.

"You lot better keep your mouths well and truly shut about the kid," said Billy. "Don't worry man, no way am I going to open my trap and have the cops all over me," said Jimmy. The two girls were silent for a while and then Jenny said, "I'm not saying a word." "Me neither," said Mavis with tears in her eyes for her lost baby. "And you can stop all your blubbering about the baby, Mavis, or someone might get the wrong idea," said Jimmy in a threatening tone of voice. "We should have kept the silver baby rattle," said Billy. "We could have flogged it and got a bob or two for it," he added. "Yeah, and maybe the cops might have led it to us you moron," his mate replied.

"What about that big reward, asked Billy. They read about it in the local newspaper. "Don't be an idiot, Billy. Trying to get the reward might also set the cops onto us you fool," replied Jimmy. "Yeah, I guess so, but the money would be good," replied Billy, always thinking about making a fast bob.

Chapter 4

The day after the rodeo, April and Thomas received an early morning visit from the local police. Still beside themselves with grief, the couple tried desperately to hold themselves together to listen to what the men were saying. Naturally they did not get any sleep. Thomas made coffee for themselves and the police. They were too upset to eat any breakfast.

Well, the search of the area and town has not revealed anything," said Constable Breen." We have searched every inch of the rodeo site and all of the shops and pubs in town," he added. "The search in the bushland will continue," he said.

"We will now commence further interviews with the townspeople to see if anyone has seen or heard anything. Following those interviews, we will contact other police districts and make up flyers to distribute around this town and in nearby towns," he added. "We will need an up-to-date photograph of your daughter," said Constable Breen to April.

April went to look for photographs with tears streaming down her face. She found one which was taken a week ago. It was a lovely photograph of Trinity in a new floral dress, showing off her curly hair and blue eyes. Just looking at it made her feel incredibly sad.

Search teams had continued well into the night and were renewed again at first light the next morning. There was no sign of the baby or any clothing which may have given them a clue. In fact, they had absolutely no idea where the child was or who might have taken her.

The police interviewed the parents at length, asking them all kinds of questions. "Did you have any enemies, disgruntled workers on the farm, students at school, people who might be jealous of you?" These were among hundreds of questions asked by the police of the distressed couple.

"You know that the press has got hold of it," said the younger policeman. "Yes, we do, and it is very distressing for us," replied Thomas.

"I get the feeling the police might suspect us," announced April one day. "Yes April, I too have been getting the same vibes from them, but I guess they just have to rule us out as suspects," he answered. "I think the police always suspect the family in the first instance," Thomas added.

The police searched their home, taking out drawers and searching wardrobes and bookcases. They even looked in the washing machine, dryer, and dishwasher plus all of the surrounding sheds, finding nothing in any of the farm buildings. They did not really expect to find anything but needed to be sure.

April and Thomas dealt with the mess left by the police, with help from some of April's friends as they put clothes away in drawers and pots and pans back into cupboards.

By lunchtime the next day, the police decided they were probably looking at a child abduction, in fact they were certain of it.

Unfortunately, after interviewing hundreds of people at the Rodeo and in the town, they were no closer to finding the little girl. One of the difficulties they ran into was the fact that many of the rodeo visitors were from out of town and therefore hard to contact.

The police turned up at the homes of Jimmy and Billy to see where they were on the day and night of the abduction. Both of them thought of prearranged answers, ready if they were questioned. From past experience they knew the police would be onto them from the start.

"Where were you boys on the day and night of the Rodeo, "the older policeman asked. "Just chilling, mate," replied Jimmy, as cheeky as ever. Billy gave the same stupid answer. "Well don't leave town in case we need to question you again." The older policeman said, "I don't think those two would have the brains to carry out a kidnapping." "Yep, I agree," said the younger man. "I don't think they have any brains at all," he added.

Trinity Jessica Louise

The police also questioned Jenny and Mavis, since they knew the four of them hung out together. Jenny denied even being with the boys, while Mavis, who was still upset about losing "her baby", pretended that she was suffering from a bad cold and started sniffing and coughing for effect. "I am really sick. I can't talk," said Mavis." I'm too ill to talk about anything," Mavis said. "We don't hang around those two idiots anymore, "said Jenny. "They are losers, those two," she added.

The police in Springfield waited for a ransom demand. They expected it, due to the Langleys being a wealthy family. As the days went into weeks, the police concluded that there was not going to be any demand for money. They formed a theory of a mother having lost a child recently, needing to fill her needs with someone else's child. They visited the local hospital and medical centres to see if anyone who recently lost a baby though a miscarriage or gave birth to a baby who died. They did not get any answers from that particular theory.

Family and friends tried to reassure and comfort Thomas and April as best as they could. Food parcels and flowers began to arrive to the popular couple. Nothing and no-one could help them with the intense grief which they felt. They tried to think positively, even though it was difficult, but as the hours moved into days, they felt less confident.

April and Thomas received a visit from their minister, Reverend Lycett who had baptised Trinity only a few months ago. "Try not to give up hope, my dears. We must put our trust in The Lord," said the Reverend. "We will try, Reverend Lycett, but it is not easy," said April sadly.

Activities around the farm continued. Animals needed to be fed and cared for, crops needed to be harvested and sheep shorn.

April took time off from her teaching duties. She could not concentrate very well, and she knew it must have been affecting her teaching.

After three months of no news of any kind, April visited her family doctor who advised her to go back to work. She was reluctant at first, but the school was understaffed, and she knew moping around the house, going in and out of her daughter's room each and every day, was only increasing her depression. The house held so many memories of her daughter, so she decided she was better off not being there as much, and she might as well be doing something useful. When she was home, April spent as much time as possible outside, only staying inside to prepare meals and clean the house. Without her little daughter, April was now left with a lot of time on her hands.

After a few weeks, things started to feel just a tiny bit better. There was always something happening around the farm and April found herself constantly wondering what her baby girl was doing, providing, she was still alive. She truly believed her daughter was still alive. "I would know if she died. I would feel it in my heart," she said.

Thomas was always a hardworking man at any time, but now he worked even harder in an attempt to stop thinking about his little girl, his little bundle of joy, remembering her cheeky smile and gurgling little laugh.

Six months after the abduction the police made a visit to the farm to inform the couple, they were no longer actively looking for their daughter. "We will still leave the case open. We have not even received one single clue," said the older policeman." "We now have other more urgent cases which need our full attention. I am so sorry," he said.

"Mr. and Mrs. Langley, our search has taken us many hours of manpower. We have searched the entire town and other police stations in NSW have all been notified. We put up flyers here and in nearby towns. The local bushlands were searched over and over. We responded to thousands of phone calls and tip offs, but unfortunately, we have found nothing. At this stage we feel there is nothing more we can do unless we get some new information. Whoever did this is either incredibly clever or extremely lucky," said the younger policeman.

April and Thomas could barely hold in their feelings of disappointment.

When they left Thomas thumped his hand against the wall and yelled "Our daughter is now a case, and not just a case, but a cold case."

Chapter 5

Some months after the kidnapping April was still going to counselling. She was also supported by her colleagues at work and close friends. Women were able to talk about things easier than men she thought. She was lucky to have several close friends to comfort her. April needed her counselling sessions just to get through the days, and especially the nights, when she lay awake for hours.

It was different for Thomas. He worked mostly alone on the farm, apart from the days when he needed help from a casual farm labourer and refused to go to counselling. He became more and more depressed as the weeks, then months went by. April knew he was not coping, and tried to get him to see a psychologist, but he refused. She became very worried about him. He was losing weight, was tired all of the time and was not sleeping. She could hear him tossing and turning in bed at night.

He felt he was losing his concentration at times and started having some nausea and dizzy spells, but he did not tell April. He knew what April would say if she found out. Each day he was feeling worse and worse, until one day, while working on the farm, he took the tractor out to the most distant paddock, and as he was going over a small rise, he rolled the tractor which slipped down the rough edge of the narrow path, leaving Thomas trapped underneath it, bleeding profusely. Thomas was working alone as his farm labourer phoned in sick. He was used to taking the tractor on this route as he did many times before.

When Thomas did not appear for dinner at the usual time, April called her neighbour Hugh Beaumont to look for him. "I saw him take the tractor out to the far paddock this morning, so I will start there. I did not see him return with the tractor," he said in a worried tone of voice.

Soon Hugh found Thomas, underneath the tractor, badly injured, having lost a lot of blood, but still conscious. He immediately called the ambulance and tried to help Thomas by wrapping his leg in an old towel and talking to him softly. The ambulance arrived fifteen minutes later and took him straight away to the local hospital where he was assessed, given a blood transfusion and then transferred immediately by air ambulance to Sydney. April raced into her car and went to the Sydney hospital immediately after calling her in-laws. She was terribly upset and blamed herself for not looking for Thomas sooner in the day.

April followed to Sydney, going as fast as speed would allow in her car, after being reassured by her in-laws they would stay at the farm as long as necessary. "I feel really bad," she told her in-laws. Thomas's parents offered to stay at the farm for as long as was needed. "You must not blame yourself, April. We all knew that Thomas was not coping, but we could not get him to see a specialist," said Mrs. Langley senior.

When April arrived in Sydney, Thomas was still in surgery. April waited anxiously for hours in the visitor's lounge to hear any news. Finally, the doctor came out and listed his multiple injuries, which included a ruptured spleen, broken ribs, a broken leg and many cuts and bruises, while assuring her he expected Thomas to make a good recovery in time. For the immediate future he would require careful nursing to prevent any infection setting in. He would also need to go to a rehabilitation centre for further physiotherapy before he could return home.

April rented a small flat near the hospital in order to be close to Thomas. She walked into a nearby church to give thanks. "I simply cannot lose you too, Thomas," she said tearfully.

April stayed with Thomas for weeks, sitting beside his bed, helping him with his meals, and reading the daily newspaper to him, as well as keeping him updated on what was happening back home at the farm. When he was allowed home after eight weeks in hospital and rehabilitation, she made sure she knew all of the exercises he was required to do each day, so she could assist him when they returned home. Thomas was very happy to go home at long last. His time in the hospital was a wake-up call for him. He knew that he should now accept some counselling.

"Please don't give me such a terrible fright ever again. I love you too much to lose you as well," said April, firmly to her husband. "I promise to be more careful, April. I am so sorry to have worried you. I knew I was not my usual self, but I really didn't think I was too bad," he replied seriously.

Following Thomas's accident, April and Thomas decided to employ a private investigator to try to find their missing daughter. The police were very thorough and did the best they could with limited resources, but the couple thought perhaps they might have missed something.

They went to visit their lawyer, Bruce Wyman who made their wills and handled any matters dealing with the property, for his advice as to who they might get to investigate Trinity's disappearance, since the police decided the case was now a cold case.

Bruce knew of two people who worked for him before. Either one would be suitable. "The costs will be high," said Bruce. "Yes, we know it will be expensive, but we need to do it," replied Thomas.

Thomas contacted the first name on the list, a man called Rod Turner and organised for him to come to their home to discuss the job the next day. Rod turned out to be a pleasant man, aged about thirty-five, who was once a policeman until he was hurt on the job and needed to retire from the force. Rod knew about the disappearance of baby Trinity and promised to do his best, although he did say they did not have much to go on.

Thomas and April were happy to be doing something positive in their search for their daughter.

Three months later Rod reported back to them that he unfortunately was not making any headway in his search for the baby. He believed whoever took Trinty probably moved as far away from the town of Springfield as possible. Rod visited all of the hospitals and medical centres to see if a baby aged around Trinity's age was ever treated there. He searched childcare centres and checked up on all child-minding places in the district. Nothing stood out as being unusual. Rod searched in nearby small towns as well.

April and Thomas asked him to continue his search for another six months, even though it did not sound very promising.

At the end of the six months, there were still no answers.

April and Thomas did not give up in their search for Trinity. They visited the police station regularly to find out if there were any updates. They also continued to check nurseries and private childcare establishments, then later primary schools in the district to find a child that looked like what they believed their daughter would look now. There were no blue eyed blonde little girls who matched Trinity's physical appearance. Whenever a new family came to town, April would visit pretending to be a welcoming visitor for the town of Springfield, in order to check if the families had any children. She and Thomas looked at every child in the Main Street of the town, always with the hope of one day seeing their beautiful little girl.

They knew what they were doing might seem a little crazy to some people, especially since the police thought the child was obviously taken away to a different area of the state, or even out of the state. April and Thomas did not give up. They were determined to find answers. They kept looking and looking, anywhere and everywhere.

Chapter 6

Jess and Will Bloom lived together as husband and wife in a weatherboard cottage on a small hobby farm with just a few acres, just outside of the town of Brinkley, about 40 kilometres from the town of Springfield. Brinkley was typical of small towns in Australia. It consisted of two pubs, a pharmacy, a doctor's surgery, small hospital and an assortment of small shops as well as two supermarkets. There was a swimming pool and gym as well as a bowling green and a golf course. There was also a railway station, with daily trains to and from Sydney.

Jess was now forty-six years old although she looked younger, and Will was almost fifty. Will was a large man with brown hair and warm brown eyes, and Jess was a slim woman with blue eyes and blonde hair, now with just a touch of grey appearing. They purchased the house and surrounding acres, after seeing an advertisement in the Weekly Times newspaper some months ago.

Will and Jess, both single, first met in their local greengrocers shop twenty years ago and through their cheerful discussions about the prices of the fruit and vegetables, formed a friendship which led to a marriage two years later, at a registry office in Sydney, where they wanted only two witnesses. They did not go anywhere for their honeymoon, just treated it as another normal day. Will and Jess's marriage was good, with both of them being content with their lives, except for one thing. Their biggest regret was not being able to have children, which disappointed them both. Over the years they both reluctantly went through a lot of testing, but doctors could not find any reason why they were not able to have children. They were told to relax and wait. After the years went by, Jess and Will finally accepted the truth, they were not ever going to have a child.

When Jess was left a vast sum of money from her aunt, Will and Jess decided to move to the country to buy a small farm. They searched for ages, looking each week in the Weekly Times newspaper until they found exactly what they wanted just outside the small country town of Brinkley.

When they first saw the house, Jess fell in love with it immediately and Will was impressed with the huge sheds which surrounded the house. It was also a very good price.

The home was built in the 1930's and it was typical of the Australian version of the Californian bungalow, with wide verandas around the home. A beautiful garden surrounded the house. The house consisted of three large bedrooms, two bathrooms and a big country kitchen with a wood stove as well as an electric stove. There were lots of outbuildings as well. Will loved his tractor and his ute, whilst Jess owned her reliable small second-hand Japanese car. Jess was proud of her lovely rose garden and Will enjoyed his vegetable patch. In the comfortable lounge room was a large fireplace where redgum logs burned in the winter. Jess and Will put all of their energy into improving their home and surroundings.

Will and Jess were friendly people, however they valued their privacy and did not socialise with neighbours, even though they received many invitations to barbeques and local parties. Jess took some of her vegetables and home-made bread to neighbours, leaving the goods at the main gate, but never went into the house when she was invited to morning tea or lunch. Their neighbours left them alone, thinking they were just very private people.

After doing all the farm chores and feeding the animals, it was their custom to have the main meal at around six P.M. and then retiring to the cosy loungeroom to watch their favourite English comedies on television, or play board games until they went to bed at around 8.30 pm. They went to bed at an early time, so that Will could rise around dawn to take care of the animals in the mornings. Jess loved her jigsaw puzzles which she did on the large dining room table, while Will enjoyed his Weekly Times newspaper, reading it from cover to cover. Sometimes Jess would spend an hour or two playing the piano or the violin. Her mother was once a beautiful pianist, and taught Jess to play the piano and the violin at an early age. They liked the town of Brinkley because it had a good rail service and hospital as well as some decent grocery and meat shops The town was very pretty, due in part to the local council planting years ago, of beautiful trees and shrubs throughout the town. There were small lagoons throughout the town, where ducks swam, and water lilies sprouted in shades of pink and yellow.

Jess liked to browse opportunity shops for her clothes. Both she and Will never bought any new clothes or shoes. It was not a matter of recycling, but rather of saving money. Neither of them liked to waste money on frivolous items. It probably related to the way in which they were brought up, as neither of them came from wealthy families, both learning to budget at an early age. Jess's mother was a single mum, since her husband walked out on her when Jess was three years old. She obtained work doing cleaning jobs in offices. Will's parents owned a small milk bar in the city, which he worked in after school. They never went without, but always needed to watch their spending. Both sets of parents were now deceased.

In spite of their recent influx of wealth, Jess and Will lived a simple life. Jessie tended her rose garden and managed her chooks and Will put in a few crops each year. They did not socialise at all, preferring to spend their time at home, in the garden or with their animals.

Their only luxury in the house was a large old piano which Jess played beautifully most evenings. She also inherited a lovely ancient violin from her aunt. They sat on a well-worn leather lounge and slept in a large pine bed, which used to belong to Will's mother.

They bought a milking cow so Jess could make her own butter from the cream. Nothing was ever wasted in the Bloom household. Jess even used the fat rendered from the meat to make her own soap. Jessica would bake her own bread every second evening.

One night just as they were about to retire for the night following Will's favourite meal which was roast beef with Yorkshire pudding with rice pudding for dessert, Jess stood up and said "Will, did you hear that noise?" "What noise," he asked. "It sounded like a kitten," she added, thinking she would like a little kitten. Both of them loved animals.

Will got up and went to the front door, to check out the soft noise, which they could only just hear.

Jess followed him and stared in amazement at the sight in front of her. Her large burly husband was holding a tiny child who was crying softly. "Oh, my goodness, what on earth do you have there," she exclaimed. "Is it what I think it is?" she added. "Yes, it is. She was lying on the front door mat," replied Will, still stunned at what he found when he opened the front door, expecting to find a kitten, not a baby.

They hurried inside and Jess took the baby from her husband. The child was dressed in a pale pink jumpsuit and wrapped in a pink knitted shawl, so they knew she was a girl. "Poor little pet, she must be so hungry," Jess said. There was a blue soft toy bunny tucked under her arm and a silver rattle which fell out of the shawl. The baby looked to be about nine months old. She was a beautiful child with blue/ grey sparkling eyes and blonde curls.

Will went outside with a torch and looked all around the house and property, walking as far as the main gate to the farm. "No one there," he said on his return. "No cars, nothing," he added.

Not sure what to do, Jess warmed some milk in a saucepan and the child drank it from a plastic mug. They were not sure if she was old enough to drink from a cup but gave it a try. They fed her some left-over custard which she loved, then propped her up on the lounge beside them surrounded by soft cushions.

"This child is starving, Will" announced Jess as she watched the child lapping up the custard. "I wonder who owns her, or why she was dumped on our doorstep," replied Will. "Perhaps her mother could not afford to keep her, and decided to leave her somewhere," replied Jess. "Yes, maybe, but don't babies get dropped off at churches or hospitals usually," said Will.

"I think she looks to be about nine to twelve months old," said Jess. "She appears to be in good health and well looked after, so I don't think she has come from a poor house or that she has not been loved," added Jess. "We need to find some sort of a bed for her," said Will.

They put her to bed in a large drawer from the hall cupboard, lined with soft cushions and a cover with a homemade quilted blanket, where she fell sleep almost immediately. They placed the blue fur bunny in the drawer beside her. Will and Jess decided to wait until the morning to make any major decisions about what to do with the little girl. "It's too late now to take her anywhere at this time of night," said Jess. "I think it will be best to just let her sleep here for tonight" said Will. "Yes, she does seem very tired, poor little pet" agreed Jess.

When morning came, Will got up early as usual and checked on the infant who was still asleep. He then took some hay to the horses. Jess went outside to feed the chooks and other animals, then made porridge and bacon and eggs for Will for his breakfast. In the meantime, the baby woke up and started to cry softly. Jess removed her from her little bed and brought her to the table where she fed her porridge and warm milk from a plastic mug. The baby loved the porridge, so Jess gave her some more. She was still very hungry. Jess tore up some old towels to make nappies for the baby.

Will watched the scene and said, "You know Jess, the little girl looks like you, with her blonde curls and blue eyes. You could be her mother."

"I would love to be her mother," replied Jess, longingly.

Will and Jess sat down on their old couch and tried to figure out what to do about the baby. "Should we go to the police, Will?" asked Jess. Will was not too keen. "No, I don't think so, at least not yet. If we go to the police, they might place her in foster care," he said. "Yes, that is true, and it would be simply awful," Jessica replied. They decided to wait until there was news of a missing child but would not go to the police just now. In the meantime, they would continue to look after the child as best they could. Underneath, Jess was keen to keep quiet about the child, in order for them to keep her. Jess desperately wanted a child to love and care for. Will also wanted to keep the child but was worried the police might think they kidnapped her, if they found out about her being with them.

"I wonder why she was dropped off here?" asked Will seriously. "We might never know," replied Jess, thoughtfully. "Perhaps because we are a bit isolated," suggested Will. "Well, we are not at all close to our neighbours or to town, so perhaps the person wanted to drop her off to somewhere isolated," said Will.

"We need to give her a name," said Will. "Yes, let's do that," replied his wife. "How about we call her Jessica, after my mum and me, and make Louise her second name after your mother," suggested Jess. Will liked the idea. Will also wanted to keep the little girl for his wife. He could see the longing look in his wife's eyes. He always knew how much she wanted a baby and how much she never talked about it.

Will and Jess decided to try to keep the baby a secret for now, and then later they could say she was their adopted daughter.

Over the next few days, the couple heard nothing about a missing child, although they didn't watch the news much on television and they rarely bought a newspaper. There was no need to go to town for at least a month or six weeks. Jessica settled in well. She was a delightful little girl, happy and cheerful and did not appear to be missing her parents. The little child was not yet walking so they carried her everywhere. Will made up a canvas sling for Jess to carry her around. Jess used her old treadle sewing machine to sew up some baby nighties and little dresses cut out from old clothes of her own. She made baby singlets out of Will's tired old worn singlets.

The days became weeks and then months, with Jess and Will rarely leaving the house or farm. When they did need groceries, Will went to town to do the shopping, while Jess stayed home with their new daughter. They were not close to their neighbours and knew only a few friends in town, so they were able to keep Jessica's arrival unnoticed. They became very absorbed in caring for the little child who was fast becoming the most important person in their once lonely lives. When she was there about three months, the child began to walk, much to the delight of her new parents. "Will, come quick. I think Jessica is standing up alone and trying to walk," she yelled to Will who was coming out of the milking shed. "Oh, how wonderful," he replied as they watched little Jessica take her first steps.

Jess not only played the piano but also sang with a beautiful voice, which delighted Jessica as her new "mother" sang lullabies to her at bedtime. Jess remembered them from her own childhood. Her favourite was Braham's Lullaby, which included the words which her own mother used.

"Lullaby and good night,

You're your mother's delight, Little angels beside.

My darling abides.

Safe and warm is your bed,

Close your eyes and lay your head.

Although very inexperienced in bringing up a child, somehow Jess and Will muddled through, due in part to the personality of the little girl. She was so happy and contented, which made caring for her a joy rather than a chore. She was also a great sleeper which was good news to her new parents.

Jess found a book on child rearing at the local newsagents which gave them some idea as to what to expect as the baby grew. "Are you having a baby, Mrs. Bloom?" asked the shop assistant. "No, dear, I will be minding a child for my sister shortly," replied Jess with a smile. Jess hurried out of the shop already regretting her decision to buy the book, in case the shop assistant did not believe her and turned her in to the police.

As time went on, Jess realised that they would need to go to town and take Jessica to the doctor for a check-up and to the community nurse to assess her development. Jess had no idea about child development. They did not think that Jessica needed a doctor, but simply wanted reassurance that they were doing all the right things for her. The doctor readily accepted the adoption story which the couple made up to cover the child's arrival. He examined Jessica and found her to be in perfect health. The nurse however asked a lot more questions. Jess told her that they adopted the child through a private adoption service, and she would bring the appropriate documents in later. The nurse also asked for Jess to bring in her immunisation records to see if they were up to date.

Jess decided then and there that she would not be going back to the same community nurse again. Jess was not particularly keen on injections for herself and felt the same about her new baby receiving them. Being a new mother with no-one to guide her, Jess did not understand the importance of immunisations. Besides which, Jess was wary about telling people in authority too much information. "That nurse was too nosey, and she was very bossy," she complained to Will. "Well, don't go back to her then," replied Will, calmly.

Later, the community nurse asked the doctor if he had seen the Bloom family, as she needed to view the immunisation records of the baby Jessica. "No, I have not seen them since the one day they came in," he replied. "Do you have their address. I will pay them a home visit?" asked the nurse. "I will check," said the doctor. When the doctor asked his assistant for the address, she said that Mrs. Bloom did not fill in any of the forms which she asked her to. "How strange. Do you know where they live?" he asked. His nurse did not have any idea. "The Blooms are not listed in the telephone book," she told the doctor.

The two shopkeepers known to Jess and Will, Peter and Wendy Mills, readily accepted the story of an adoption, talking gently to the little girl as she sat in her new stroller. Wendy tried to find out where the child had come from, but Jess shut down, refusing to answer and left the shop, going quickly to her car.

Jess and Will recently purchased a cot, baby bath and other baby items from the second-hand furniture shop in town. Jess purchased lots of baby clothes from the opportunity shop. Jessica was having a growth spurt and was now walking everywhere, even chasing the chooks, which delighted her new temporary parents. They also went to a second opportunity shop at which Jess shopped often, to buy even more baby items.

Jessica had plenty of clothes even if they were second hand.

They thought she was about sixteen months old now. Will and Jess decided to visit their lawyer, old Mr. Lawson, to see if it would be possible to get a birth certificate made up. Will heard someone in the supermarket saying Mr. Lawson was having money worries. Mr. Lawson did not ask them why they needed a new birth certificate. They made up a story about having lost the original certificate and offered the lawyer a large sum of money to create a new one.

Their lawyer was open to the suggestion of a decent amount of money changing hands for the birth certificate and before too long, they were able to hold the certificate in their hands. Only they and Mr. Lawson knew the truth. Their lawyer was a known gambler and was running short of cash due to his unwise gambling efforts. He would do anything to save his wife and son from the disgrace of bankruptcy. The offer of ready cash was too tempting to knock back. Naturally Mr. Lawson made them sign an agreement about the deal. He too wanted the matter to remain a secret.

One day when Jess and Will decided to shop together and to take little Jessica in her push chair, a total stranger came up to the three of them and said, "Your little girl looks very much like a baby I used to know. Is she adopted?" she asked. Will became very annoyed and said, "Of course not, can't you see she is the image of her mother." "Yes, I do see that now, I apologise," the woman said and went on her way, thinking they were a strange couple and very touchy.

"You see now, Jess, why we can't bring her into town until she is older," said Will, anxiously. "Yes, it is too much of a risk," replied Jess.

The incident frightened Jess and Will, who became even more determined to keep their new daughter out of the public eye, at least until she was much older. Jess even decided to hang the baby's washing in the shed to avoid prying eyes.

"Should we get her baptised," Jess suggested to Will one day. "It would be nice, but too risky, I think, as much as I would like to," he replied.

Chapter 7

In the meantime, back at the home of April and Thomas, life settled into a very different style. Instead of waking up each day to feed and play with their little girl, they now took breakfast alone together, and without their little girl. Their lives were simply not the same. They missed her gentle laugh and funny little ways. They struggled to come to terms with the loss of their little baby, Trinity. Thomas took on new roles as CEO of the local building society and secretary of the show committee to try to fill his days, whilst April took up quilting and went to advanced cooking classes, both of them trying to fill their lives with numerous activities in order to stop thinking about their lost child.

As time went on, they decided to try for another baby, not to replace their daughter but they always wanted more children, so it seemed logical.

They finally accepted that their little girl was not coming home. The only thing they would have liked was closure. Even if she was dead, at least they would know, and could have a memorial service for her. As it was, they could never truly move on when they did not know if she was alive or dead.

April found it hard to be around other little children and refused all invitations to children's birthday parties in the district. Many of their friends had babies who were the same age as Trinity. April found it difficult to be with them. On Trinity's birthday each year they would have a little cup cake with candles. That was really the only thing they could do to cope with the day. They did not have a grave on which to place flowers.

April persuaded Thomas to try IVF and after two years and many rounds of treatment, April faced two miscarriages in the first trimester. The miscarriages left her depressed and weak. It became all too much, with travelling to Sydney for treatment, and the toll it took on April, so they gave the idea away deciding that if it was not meant to be, then so be it. If they managed to fall pregnant it would be a blessing, but they were not expecting it to happen. April was prepared to continue with the treatments, but Thomas was not. "It is too hard on your body, April," he said. Their grief never went away. April continued to believe that Trinity was alive. She never gave up hoping and nor did Thomas. "I truly believe I would know if she died," said April, sadly.

Chapter 8

Jessica was proving to be a very smart little girl. This was evident from the moment they first found her, so Jess decided to teach her to read when she turned three. Jess kept a lot of children's books from her own childhood and managed to find others at the local opportunity shop. She also taught her to play the piano. Jessica was an extremely keen student, always willing to face any challenge that came her way. She showed a maturity way beyond her years. She started to talk at age one, even making whole sentences.

She was now a happy, healthy little girl and very beautiful as her golden curls trailed almost near her shoulders with her blue eyes bright and shining.

When Jessica came of school age at around five, Jess and Will debated about her attending primary school. They considered home schooling as an alternative. Jessica herself made the decision to do home schooling. Jess and Will were happy with this outcome, not wanting to get involved with schools due to what information the school might wish to know. "Do you want to go to big school or stay here with mummy and daddy?" April asked her one day. "I don't want to leave you and daddy," she replied. Will and Jess breathed a huge sigh of relief.

Jess felt confident she could teach Jessica at home. Even though Jess grew up in a poor household, her mother was very strict about Jess getting a good education, so Jess went through high school and then did a secretarial course. Her mother also wanted her to read as many books as possible, so they visited the local library often. Jess was happy, especially in summer because the library was air-conditioned, and she did not even have a fan at home.

They were constantly aware of the fact that someone might query the supposed adoption and would go to any lengths to protect themselves and the daughter they now loved so much. They would have hated it if Jessica was ever taken away from them and lived in constant fear the police might come knocking on their door on day.

"Don't you want to meet other children," they asked her, hoping that she would say no. Jessica replied, "No, mother, I do meet other children at pony club and Sunday school, and I really am happiest when I'm here at home with you both." Jessica was a well-loved cheerful little girl. She was a good eater, enjoying fresh food from the farm each day and doing her daily chores such as feeding the chooks, her pet lamb and looking after her pony named Tilly. She was accepted by only a few people who knew her family, as the adopted daughter of Jess and Will Bloom.

Jess reluctantly allowed Jessica to go to pony club on Saturday afternoons with her pony, Tilly. They did not stay for afternoon tea. "Mummy, why can't we stay?"

begged her daughter repeatedly. Jess always used the excuse of needing to go home to feed the animals.

It was the same with Sunday School. Jessica was whisked away as soon as the class finished, and they never stayed for morning tea after church. "We have work to do on the farm," said Will.

They decided not to tell Jessica about her "adoption" or the facts surrounding it. "There is absolutely no need for Jessica to ever know anything about her background or where she came from," said Jess. "I totally agree," replied her husband. "It might upset her, or she might try to find her biological parents" he added. "You know how clever she is," he said.

Jessica showed an exceptional ability in the area of music. Already an accomplished pianist at age five, she could not only sing and play the guitar, but lately was enjoying her violin lessons with her mother, playing the antique violin which belonged to Jess's mother, but still with an exceptional sound. One day Jess spoke to Will about Jessica's violin lessons. "I don't think I can teach her anymore. She needs a more professional teacher," she announced to Will. "Well, let's try and find just the right person for her. We need to encourage her as much as we can. I believe she is truly gifted," he answered.

There was a retired music professor living in town, so Jess visited him one day to talk about Jessica. His name was Professor Horton and he received Jess with some amusement, "You say your daughter is only six years old," he said. "I will listen to her and advise you, but don't expect too much as she is really far too young to have much talent," he added skeptically.

Jessica and her mother Jess made an appointment with Professor Horton for Jessica to meet with him the following week. Jess took Jessica to town one day just for a quick visit, in order to get her a dress to wear at the interview. They went to their favourite opportunity shop where the volunteer just unpacked a beautiful red dress in Jessica's size. Jessica tried it on and looking in the mirror thought it was the most beautiful dress she ever saw. "Thank you so much, mother. I really love this dress," said Jessica, enthusiastically.

Jess carried the violin in its case, and they arrived on time. Professor Horton looked at Jessica, thinking what a beautiful little girl she was. When she started to play, he was lost for words. There was no doubt in his mind that this girl was not only outwardly lovely, but extremely talented as well.

He responded by inviting them to visit a former student who was teaching privately in a large town about eighty kilometres away. "He is a brilliant young man and an excellent teacher. He was an outstanding student. He only takes a few students a week," said Professor Horton. "I believe he is exactly the right person to teach Jessica at this stage of her musical development," he added. "I will contact him for you," said Professor Horton.

All was arranged for Jessica to have her first lesson with Adam Kenty, the music teacher, at his home in a week's time. Jess drove her daughter to her first lesson, both of them a little bit apprehensive. "There is no need to be nervous, Jessica," her mother said. Adam's house was easy to find, set back in a lovely garden with many English trees.

Adam Kenty was a nice-looking man, aged about thirty-five. He had played the violin whilst in the Sydney symphony orchestra, but now taught music at his local high school since his wife developed an auto-immune disease. They moved to the country to be closer to his wife's parents so they could assist in the care of his wife.

Adam was very interested and intrigued to meet the six-year-old violinist. He greeted them warmly and took Jessica into his music room whilst Jess waited in the kitchen, where Adam's wife offered her a cup of tea. "I would really love to play in the Sydney symphony orchestra when I grow up," said Jessica. Adam was amused at her confidence. He was both surprised and amazed at Jessica's first performance for him. "This girl has real talent," he told his wife. "I have never heard a child with such potential," he added. It was agreed that Jessica would attend for a long lesson, once a week from then on. Over the next few months and years, Jess happily drove Jessica to Adam's house for her violin lessons. She was a much more polished violinist by then, at only ten years old.

When Jessica was twelve her parents again debated where to send her for her high school studies. Her grades were outstanding, but they worried about whether she should go to the local high school, or to a Sydney boarding school for girls. They did not want to send her away to a Sydney school, but at the same time wanted her to get a good education. Many local children went away to boarding school.

"I want to stay close to you both," Jessica announced to her parents. At the back of Jessica's mind was the high cost of boarding school. She did not want her parents to have to go without, just so they could pay the private school fees, but she never told them her reason. And so, it was decided she would attend the local high school, travelling on the bus each day with other students. Will and Jess were happy to know she chose to go to school locally, feeling more secure in knowing she was nearby. They did not want her to out of their sight for too long even though she was now twelve years old.

Jessica enjoyed high school and naturally excelled at all of her subjects, including music. She particularly loved ancient history and French lessons. By now Jessica progressed further than Adam could take her with violin lessons, but she still continued to practice both the piano and violin for hours at a time. She did not regard it as practice, rather she thought of it as fun and pleasure.

Jessica was blessed with many friends, although her parents did not encourage sleepovers, so her contact with them was mainly on the bus or at school. She did not understand why her parents kept to themselves so much and were so overprotective of her. It was not as if she was a sickly child or needed extra care. All of her friends were allowed much more freedom. They went to sleepovers and shopping in town with friends.

Chapter 9

Jessica grew up to be a well-mannered young lady with a charming nature. She enjoyed talking to her friends at school about many different topics. At home her mother shared her cooking secrets. "I just love cooking with you, mother," Jessica said one day. Equally, she also enjoyed working in her father's shed. Will was very clever with wood and taught Jessica to make household objects from old timber found around the farm. Jessica was very respectful of others and was a kind friendly girl.

The years passed quickly and before long Jessica completed high school and was sitting for her final examinations. Her final year was very busy with the extra study required but Jessica sailed through it with confidence. She was then considering her offers to various universities around the country including those which offered music as a main subject choice.

"I really want to study music" she told her parents. It was no surprise to them. She ended up being dux of the school which delighted her parents, Will and Jess, who proudly clapped at her valedictorian celebration. "We did good, Jess," said Will, filled with pride. "I believe so, my dear," replied Jess with tears in her eyes. It was one of the few occasions when they visited the school. Staying away from school events meant staying safe for Will and Jess. They were always worried in case one day someone would find out the truth and come looking for their daughter. The fear never left them even though it was now eighteen years since she arrived as a baby on their front door mat.

Then began a rush of interviews at various universities for Jessica. It was an exciting time for her. She insisted on doing them alone, not wanting her parents to leave the farm too much, so travelled by train or bus to the city. Jessica felt that it was time for her to start to become more independent and not to be so reliant on her parents.

Her parents were reluctant for her to go on her own, but she managed to talk them into it. "I need to start doing things on my own and to become more self-reliant," she said gently. "Besides, next year when I go to University, I will have to be on my own to fend for myself," she added. Truthfully her parents did not like being out with Jessica too much in case someone recognized either her or them, even though it was years since she had become their daughter.

They decided it was better and safer this way. Jessica, however, was always thinking of the added costs if her parents travelled with her. Jessica travelled to Sydney by train, managing very well on her own. She phoned her parents every night with an update on her interviews.

They were going well, and Jessica was confident that she would get accepted into the university of her choice. Music was always at the forefront of her mind.

Jessica loved her time in the big city. She was fascinated with the Opera House and the Harbour Bridge. "I would love to play my violin at the Opera House one day," she told her parents, on the phone one night. Jess said, "We will be very proud to see you do it. We have absolutely no doubts at all you will do it," replied her mother with pride in her voice.

Jessica was staying at a small inexpensive boutique hotel in Sydney and was alone when she received a phone call from the police from her hometown. She thought the call was from her mother or father as she felt no-one else would know where she was. She answered the call which was from the Brinkley police station. They tracked her down through information which Jess left at the house. She wondered why on earth would the Brinkley police be calling her. She didn't for one minute think it would be anything bad. Nothing could have prepared her for the enormous shock which she was about to receive.

It was a single vehicle accident. The car slipped down an embankment on a poorly lit road at sundown, only a few kilometres from their home during a bad storm. The road was full of potholes and many people reported it to the local council over the past few months. The small car was a total write-off. Some neighbours witnessed the accident. "There was nothing we could do," said Bill Stevens, one of the neighbours. The couple were on their way home after grocery shopping in town, to get a leg of lamb for Jessica's homecoming meal. Both Jess and Will were killed instantly.

Jessica struggled with the news of her parents' deaths. "I just can't believe it," she told the policeman who phoned her. "Are you sure it was my parents in the accident?" she asked. "Yes, my dear, a neighbour who found them said there was no doubt," replied the policeman, gently.

Jessica was suffering from shock, all by herself in her hotel room. There was no-one to comfort her. She curled up on her bed in a large blanket and sobbed her eyes out There was nothing she could do until morning. The next day Jessica went home on the train, never having felt so alone before in her life. She could not believe her loving wonderful parents were really gone. The hotel manager took her a cup of tea and sandwiches and offered to drive her to the station the next day before she went home.

Jessica went straight to the local hospital on her return, to see her parents, even though the police advised her they did not think it was a good idea, because of their extensive injuries. However, Jessica needed to say goodbye to them. It was not a pleasant task for anyone, especially an eighteen-year-old girl. Jessica remained strong and calm throughout the viewing but broke down as soon as she left the hospital. She sat in her father's old ute, trying to make sense out of what happened to her parents. Fortunately, their faces were not too badly injured.

A week later, Jessica stood at the front of the church where her parents once worshiped, and played her violin, a lovely tune which was a particular favourite of her mother's. It was by Bach: Chaconne in D-minor, which Bach had written when his first wife died when he was travelling. Jessica played the piece for fifteen minutes, managing to get through the whole piece without breaking down.

The church was packed with community members, most of whom Jessica did not know. A few of her school friends and Adam, her music teacher was also present. Her parents chose to lead a sheltered life, but the community always gathered for funerals of accident victims, even if they were not known to them.

As Jessica left the church and made her way to the local lawn cemetery, she was deep in thought, not truly understanding the enormity of her loss as yet. There were only a few people near the grave site at the local lawn cemetery. Suddenly a woman tapped her on her shoulder, and she turned to see a woman of about sixty, with glasses and short wavy hair, her build not unlike her mother Jess's shape. "Hello, Jesssica" she said. "Do I know you?" asked Jesssica, puzzled. The woman replied "No, probably not, but I am a cousin of your mother. Our mothers were sisters. I read about the accident in the newspaper and even though I have not seen your mother for many years, I remember spending a lot of time with Jess when we were children. I wanted to be here today." "Thank you for coming. I did not realise my mother knew any relatives still living. She never mentioned you." said Jessica. "Well to be honest, I did not know Jess and Will were blessed with a child. As I said, it has been a long time since we have been in touch."

Her name was Roslyn Myer. She lived in the city and just recently retired from her long-time job as a medical assistant in a small family practice. She gave Jessica her phone number and told her to call if ever she needed a friend or a shoulder to cry on. Jessica thought Roslyn was a lovely woman, and it was good to know that she was blessed with some family at last, if she ever needed to call anyone.

Roslyn left then, kissing Jessica goodbye. Jessica was left with the daunting task of hosting a wake which was held in the church hall. After shaking what felt like hundreds of hands, and talking to all and sundry, finally Jessica left the hall and headed home to her empty house, dreading walking into the home which no longer held her beloved parents. Jessica was grateful to the townspeople who came out in force to pay their respects, especially because she knew that her parents did not involve themselves very much at all in the community.

When Jessica arrived home, she went to feed the chooks and animals and spent some time with her lovely old pony, Tilly, cuddling into her neck, seeking the comfort which only animals can give.

There was plenty of food at the house, thanks to the generosity of neighbours, but she did not feel hungry. At least she would not have to do grocery shopping for ages she thought.

Arriving home Jessica was immediately aware of the silence in the house. She wandered around the empty house for a while, touching the old furniture and her mother's things, such as her newly washed apron hanging near the stove, and the tea towels set out on the drying rack. Her dad's work boots stood at the back door and there was a stack of wood in the wheelbarrow ready to light the fires for the stove and open fire in the lounge. There were so many wonderful memories, Jessica did not doubt for a minute about the love her parents felt for her. Jess and Will over time, turned their house into a real family home, warm and comfortable.

When she came to her parents' bedroom where she went into so many times before, Jessica sat down at the lovely old dressing table and started to look through her mother's drawers. There were some old bills, handkerchiefs, some cuttings from newspapers and a few photographs. Also in the drawers were a few pieces of old costume jewellery and a string of pearls. Jessica took out all of the photographs and tried to figure out to whom they belonged. Most of the photos were old and faded. Jessica did not recognise anyone in them except for her parents when they were younger. She searched for photos of herself, but they were few and far between. She could not find any photographs of herself as a baby which she found strange, as most people loved taking pictures of their new babies. Nor were there many photos of her growing up.

There were earlier photos of Will and Jess prior to their marriage, and she did find one which she thought may have been taken on their wedding day as well as one or two of Jessica on her pony and on the farm, but no portraits or school photos. Jessica knew that photographs were taken of her each year at school in her school uniform. She also recalled asking her mother one day why there were no photos in frames, in the house. Her mother had replied photographs made Will feel sad, so she did not persevere with the idea even though she thought the answer was strange.

Jessica puzzled over the lack of photographs, but decided to ask their old family doctor if her knew of any reason why there would not be any baby photos of her.

Chapter 10

Jessica received a phone call from her parents' lawyer about five days after the funeral asking her to come in to see him as soon as possible. She owned a driver's license now, so drove to town in her father's old ute, which was not the safest vehicle on the road, needing lots of repairs. Her mother's car no longer existed. Jessica thought she might have to get another car when she could afford it.

Her parents' lawyer was a friendly man who began serving his community just a few short years ago. He welcomed Jessica warmly into his bright friendly office and offered his sincere condolences to her. He was the son of their previous lawyer, old Mr. Lawson who now had dementia, and could no longer practice.

Mr. Greg Lawson asked her how she was coping. He explained to her about his father now being unwell with dementia and how he decided to take over his father's law practice. He said there was not much in his father's file on the Bloom family except for the wills. Jessica asked him if there was any evidence of her being adopted and he said "No, my dear, absolutely nothing," leaving

Jessica to assume, if in fact she was adopted, then perhaps her parents' lawyer might have left some details.

"Jessica, I don't know if you are aware of it, but you are now a very wealthy young woman," Greg Lawson announced to Jessica as he read out the wills of her parents. "What do you mean, Mr. Lawson. My parents did not have much money, and lived off their own produce," Jessica replied. "No, Jessica. They lived a simple life, but were actually very wealthy people, with huge investments and enormous bank accounts as well as property in Sydney and in regional areas. They also owned a great number of residential apartments in the city. It was their choice to live a simple uncomplicated lifestyle. Your mother inherited a very large sum of money from her aunt a few years ago," said Mr. Lawson. "I had absolutely no idea, Mr. Lawson. They lived so frugally," she said. "Well, Jessica, you will never have to worry about money, as long as you live," he stated.

Jessica left Mr. Lawson's office in a state of shock. Why did her parents live such a simple life, never going on holidays or having decent cars or even the luxury of air-conditioning when they were so wealthy. She simply could not understand their reasoning. They bought their clothes at opportunity shops. The summer days were very hot, however Jess and Will used only small fans, and then only when it was extremely hot and humid. Jessica could never remember ever going to the beach, or any other holiday spots like her friends from school often talked about. She always wanted to go to the Gold Coast, having heard so much about it from her school friends.

Will's ute was probably over twenty years old and just barely getting him around, while Jess's little old car displayed hundreds of kilometres on the dial. They were always conscious of wasting water and saving electricity. Jessica simply could not understand their reasoning. She never wanted or needed anything. Her parents provided very well for her, but it would have been nice to have gone to the seaside or to somewhere like Tasmania with her parents, while they were still alive.

After going to the coffee shop for an iced coffee and a sandwich, Jessica decided to visit the family doctor. Dr. Robinson was their family doctor for years, although Jessica was a healthy child and only met him on rare occasions. Will and Jess also only visited occasionally. Someone did not turn up for an appointment, so the doctor was able to fit Jessica in.

"What can you tell me about my birth, Dr. Robinson?" she asked. "Well, Jessica, I can't tell you much really. I did not get to meet you until you were over sixteen months old, so I just assumed that Jess gave birth to you somewhere else, which did seem a bit odd to me at the time because I know she and Will had been trying for a baby for years before and I was assisting them with referrals to various doctors in the city. I would have thought Jess may have given birth to you at our local hospital. Your mother just turned up one day with you. The other strange thing I remember was our local community health nurse asking for your immunisation records, but Jess never provided them. It was all a bit of a mystery at the time," he said, shaking his head. "Another interesting thing was why Jess never completed any forms regarding your address or family details," he added.

"The reason I am asking, Dr. Robinson, is because there appear to be no photographs of me as a baby, or when I was growing up. In fact, the only recent photographs were a wedding photo and two of me on my pony" Jessica added.

"Yes, that is unusual indeed. Did you have photos taken at school?" asked Dr. Robinson. "Perhaps you might try looking for your birth certificate. A birth certificate might give you some information," he suggested. Jessica told him how she remembered being photographed at school but, there were no school photos at all in the house. She thought at the time perhaps her parents could not afford to pay for the photographs.

Jessica went home and started to look for her birth certificate in her mother's only personal file. She found it, among other papers, but there were no records of her childhood immunisations or of her baptism, which was also unexpected since her parents were church goers. Jessica wondered why her parents never took her to be baptised. They took communion every week and so did she. The family bible stood on Jess's bedside table. Jessica opened it, expecting to find family details, but there was nothing written in the front or anywhere else. She expected to find some information as most family bibles contained, but there was no writing of any kind in the book.

The birth certificate revealed nothing either. It only stated her birth at a Sydney hospital with her name and the date and year of birth which she already knew. It was a very plain birth certificate.

Jessica decided to phone her mother's cousin, whom she met at the funeral. "Hello, is it you Roslyn?" she asked. "Why Jessica dear, how are you?" Jessica told her she was fine but missing her parents a lot and she was wondering why there were no photos of her as a baby. "Yes, that is strange because Will loved to take photographs when I knew them. They sent me a wedding photograph," said Roslyn. "Yes, I found a similar one. Did you ever see me as a baby?" asked Jessica. "Well, no, I did not. I did not even know about you, until I heard on the grapevine that you were born. It was probably when you were about two by then," said Roslyn.

"It does all sound like a bit of a mystery, doesn't it," she added. "I can't understand why my mother did not tell you she gave birth to a baby. You were her only relative," added Jessica. "Roslyn, was my mother baptised?" asked Jessica. "Why yes, she was. Her mother was church going, never missed a Sunday," replied Roslyn "Do you have your birth certificate?" asked Roslyn. "Yes, nothing remarkable there," replied Jessica. "I would have thought getting you baptised was important to her and Will," added Roslyn.

They left the conversation up in the air with Roslyn promising to keep in touch especially if she found out anything of interest.

Jessica decided to forget about the issue for the time being and to try to concentrate on mapping out her future, now her parents were no longer a part of her life. There was nothing she could do about the past, but the future needed to be organized for her in order to get over her grief and move on with her life. She felt very alone during the saddest time of her life. In spite of her loss, Jessica was a strong girl, and she knew eventually she would find peace.

Chapter 11

Now she was a wealthy young woman, with a great deal of money, more than she ever thought possible, Jessica's thoughts turned to travel. She needed time to get over her loss and could not face university just yet at this time in her life.

Jessic decided to write to the university of her choice to defer her studies for a year. She did not feel as if she could concentrate on her studies while she was still grieving. Jessica never travelled out of Australia or anywhere else, except more recently to Sydney, but she felt a strong yearning to go to Europe and the British Isles to see the parts of the world where the great composers of music once lived and studied. Jessica read so much about Europe and the British Isles in school and at home, and always wondered if she would ever have the opportunity to go there. Now Jessica would have the time and the money to travel.

Jessica made a decision to lease the farm by advertising in the Weekly Times. There were several replies to her advertisement. She interviewed all of them. One couple did not like trees, which worried her.

Another family consisted of nine children, too many for the size of the house. The reply which appealed to her most was from a young couple with two small children who were keen to live in the area and practice organic farming. She leased the farm as it was, with all furniture and equipment as well. She did not need the money but wanted the farm to be treated well and respectfully, since it meant so much to her parents and it was one way she could still honour them.

The young couple needed six weeks to sell their present house in the city and Jessica was happy to oblige since she needed to do so much organizing before going overseas to start her new adventure. Her passport recently arrived in the post. Now the trip seemed very real, and she started to look forward to it.

Jessica kept only a few keepsakes from her parents' home including an antique brush and comb set and a lovely old mirror. She placed most of the things in a storage unit in Sydney. There were a couple of boxes, as well as a few pieces of antique furniture. She kept her mother's wedding ring and pearls. Jess did not seem to have much jewellery, not even an engagement ring.

Just after her nineteenth birthday, Jessica set out on her first ever flight to Europe. Her birthday was spent alone when she visited her parents' graves at the Brinkley cemetery and sat down to have a good cry. She purchased a backpack, trying hard to fit everything in and thought if she got too cold, she could always purchase warmer clothes.

Jessica took a train to Sydney, then went by taxi to Sydney airport which she thought was huge with people coming and going in all directions. Once she checked in, she was able to sit down with a cup of coffee and relax.

At the airport the large plane loomed large and almost confronting as she boarded with hundreds of other passengers for her first stop in Germany. She decided to go to Europe first and to stay in hostels, but if she felt like it, could afford to use hotels as well, or bed and breakfast accommodation.

Chapter 12

Following the "baby incident" the four teens were still living at their parents' homes in Springfield, not having done much with their lives.

It was now three years since the four teens stole the baby from the car at Springfield. By now they were three years older but no wiser.

Jenny turned out the best of the four. She was working in her parents' hardware shop and while there, fell in love, or lust with a carpenter called Douglas. Douglas worked for his father and was currently building a new house for him and Jenny. The house was a triple fronted weatherboard house in a new area of Springfield and was almost finished. Jenny bragged about her lovely new home to anyone who would listen.

Jenny was now twenty-one years old, the eldest of the four. She was busy planning her upcoming wedding. She saw in her mind visions of herself, surrounded by yards and yards of white tulle, with a long lace veil covering her head and walking down the aisle of the church, followed by her seven bridesmaids wearing bright purple

Trinity Jessica Louise

satin dresses, and carrying white lilies. Jenny loved white lilies, however she herself would be carrying white roses, a sign of purity she thought. Since she was already pregnant, there was nothing pure about Jenny. She did not dare to tell her religious parents she was having a baby. Jenny planned to have a huge bouquet with a big satin white ribbon to cover her increasing bulge. All she needed to do, was to continue to hide from her parents for just a short while longer.

Jimmy Willis and Billy Jones both got some work, although Billy recently lost his job due to a work accident which he caused and was now living on welfare from the Government. As a result of the accident Billy's workmate was now in a wheelchair, not that Billy cared too much. Jimmy managed to get a job washing windows for building firms, but when household and other things like spades and rakes, started to go missing, naturally Jimmy was the first suspect, and he was dismissed from his job. Now, he too was living on Government benefits. The two young men were still meeting up and stealing cars together. Billy received a steady income through selling prescription drugs to local teenagers. He stole them each month from his mother's supply of antidepressants and anxiety medications. Since she took so many, Billy was sure that she would never miss them, and at least it provided Billy with some money for his cigarettes and cheap alcohol, usually beer and rum.

Not surprisingly, Mavis fared the worst. She became obsessed with babies, having taken one from a pram one day and tried to run away with the child, before the mother saw her and screamed for the police. "Help, help, someone has taken my baby," the woman yelled hysterically, while trying to catch Mavis who was running down the Main Street holding tightly onto the crying baby. Mavis tried to convince the police that it was her baby.

When questioned, the policemen asked Mavis why she took the baby. "I thought it was my baby. It looked the same as my baby," she said tearfully. "Do you have a baby, Mavis," the constable asked. "I used to, but they took it," she said sadly. "Who took it?" the constable asked. Mavis did not answer. She shook her head and just sat there crying. The two men looked at each other and decided there was something wrong with the woman. They simply could not communicate with her on a normal level. They thought Mavis was probably mentally challenged and needed expert help.

Mavis was becoming a problem too, for Jimmy and Billy. Her constant ramblings about babies were giving them headaches. "We need to shut her up, or she will get us all into trouble with the cops," said Billy. "Yeah, but how?" asked his mate trying to think of a way to get rid of the tiresome woman.

"Can you get some more drugs from your old woman?" asked Jimmy. "Sure thing. It will be easy," replied Billy. "She has so many pills she won't even notice they are missing," he added.

Soon Billy secretly raided his mother's drug cupboard once again and they gathered a smorgasbord of drugs and several bottles of cheap rum and cola. They invited mad

Mavis as they called her, to meet them for a party up near the old gold mine.

Mavis arrived, muttering to herself, saying "Where is my baby" over and over. Mavis looked around and could not see anyone else. "Where is everybody?" she asked. "Coming later" replied Jimmy with a sneaky look on his face. "You are first to arrive Mavis," said Billy with a smirk.

"Want a drink, Mavis" said Billy. She replied that she would, so the boys mixed about fifteen of the crushed antidepressants into a large rum and cola, with not much cola. She gobbled it down and asked for another. She drank the very strong second rum and cola. Before long Mavis started to wobble on her feet, to stumble all over the place, and was wanting to be sick. "I feel sick. Please help me. I feel terrible," she said. Mavis wandered slowly and incoherently onto the ground, vomiting profusely.

The two louts ignored her calls for help, moving away from her then and laughing as she collapsed in a heap onto the ground. It was a very cold night, now the sun was setting, so the boys kicked her further over onto the grass, leaving her uncovered and not caring about whether she was alive or dead. They then took off in yet another stolen car to do burn outs, leaving poor Mavis in agony and struggling to breathe. They were hoping they gave her enough drugs to kill her. "What if she comes out of it and tells the cops," said Jimmy. "No way is Mavis going to wake up," replied Billy, with certainty. "We knocked her out, good and proper."

Mazi Mcburnie

The next morning Mavis's large, bloated body was found by hikers early in the morning. They called the police, but nothing could be done to save her. One of the policemen recognised her. "Isn't that old man Beatty's kid," he said.

The police visited Mavis's dad who was not surprised or upset in the least bit, when told of Mavis's death. "Always thought someone would do her in, one day. She was crazy, always going on about her lost baby. Never even gave birth to a baby that I knew of," he announced. They asked if it would be possible to look in Mavis's bedroom. Her father could not care less and took them into her room, which like the rest of the house was one big mess.

When they entered her room, the two policemen found a large number of baby items, including a baby cradle and many baby clothes, nappies and half-filled baby bottles. The baby clothes were all pink. Don Beatty could think of no reason why she would have compiled a stack of baby items in her room. He told police he never went into her room. Constable Druitt asked Don if Mavis might have been pregnant. He said he did not think so. "She would be too stupid to get herself pregnant and beside which, she has never been seen with a boyfriend," he said.

"Why on earth would the woman have all of those baby items if she had no baby?" asked Constable Druitt. "Who would know. She sounds like she may have been a bit crazy," replied the other policeman.

Trinity Jessica Louise

Billy and Jimmy received a visit from the police. "Have you boys seen Mavis Beatty lately," asked one of the policemen. "Have not seen the stupid cow for months," said Billy. "Me neither. Don't want to see her either," added Jimmy. "Did either one of you ever see Mavis with her baby?" asked one of the policemen. "A baby. Are you crazy," Billy laughed. "No sane bloke would ever go near mad Mavis," he added. "That's for sure," added Jimmy with a huge grin.

An autopsy revealed Mavis died from an overdose. They determined it to be a cocktail of drugs and alcohol which according to her dad was strange, since Mavis did not usually drink alcohol especially rum. The other matter which bothered them was where she obtained the drugs which appeared to be prescription drugs. There was no sign of pregnancy either in the past or present. The coroner decided her death was suspicious.

The case was then taken over by the local police and overseen by the state homicide division.

The local police searched the area where Mavis's body was found. They found cigarette buts and two small white tablets at the scene which they took to the local pharmacy. The pharmacist identified them as being Prozac and Mirtazapine, both commonly used anti-depressants, but was unable to tell which batch they had come from or who may have had a prescription for them. The cigarette buts were too badly soiled to get a decent fingerprint from.

Two empty rum bottles were also found at the scene. The local bottle shop manager said it was a cheap rum, often drunk by teenagers, leading them to think the deed may have been carried out by a young person or people, most likely known to the victim. The bottles were partially wiped clean.

"I think we might need to look more closely at Billy and Jimmy. They were a bit too slick with their answers," said Constable Druitt. "Maybe Jenny will know something," said Constable White. "Worth a try," replied his colleague.

The pair tried to see Jenny, however she was on her honeymoon in Queensland when they called, so it would have to wait.

Mavis was buried in a council plot at the local cemetery as her father could find no money to bury her. Very few people came to the funeral, but Jenny went since she knew her in the past and felt sorry for her family. Dressed in black and holding her large pregnant tummy in, she did not speak to Billy or Jimmy, considering herself to now be better than them. She believed she was in a different social class to the two losers. Jenny even wondered if Jimmy and Billy killed Mavis. She would not be surprised if they were the killers. Jenny knew both of the boys could exhibit an evil streak. Billy and Jimmy watched the proceedings from outside of the fence which surrounded the council section of the cemetery.

Mavis's sister Beverley and her brother Kenny attended the funeral. Her sister was crying, but her brother only went to keep up appearances. Beverley went over to where Billy and Jimmy were standing. "I bet you idiots did something to Mavis to cause her death," said

Beverley. "Get a life you moron," said Billy to Beverley, who turned and ran as fast as she could. Beverley was only fifteen and she was frightened of the two louts.

Billy and Jimmy felt no remorse. As far as they were concerned the death of Mavis was a problem solved. They were really happy to have Mavis gone from their useless lives. She could not ever bother them again. They were safe now.

Chapter 13

When Jenny returned home from her honeymoon in Queensland, she received a visit from two policemen. She was now Mrs. Jenny Moore. Jenny opened the door, dressed in a towelling bathrobe, with her baby bump showing from underneath the robe. "What can I do for you gentlemen?" she asked.

"We are looking into the death of Mavis Beatty," said Constable Druitt. "When did you last see Mavis?" asked Sargent Brown. "Oh, poor Mavis. That was so sad," said Jenny pretending to be sorry.

"I have not seen her for months, maybe years," Jenny replied. "But you were friends once," said Constable Druitt. "Not for years. Mavis went a bit crazy a while back, started doing weird things," added Jenny. "Do you know why?" asked Sergeant Brown. Jenny blushed bright red and stayed quiet for a moment. "No idea," replied Jenny. "What about this baby business?" asked Constable Druitt. Jenny went quiet again, pretending to be unsure as to what they were referring.

"I don't know what you are talking about. I know nothing about a baby," muttered Jenny, who was by now shaking like a leaf. Jenny then went from bright red to pale and asked to sit down, holding her stomach. "Do you mind, gentlemen, I am not feeling well," said Jenny, disliking the way that the conversation was heading and looking for a way out.

The two policemen looked at each other and then decided to leave the questioning for now. Clearly the mention of a baby was upsetting for Jenny, but for what reason, they did not know.

Back at the station Constable Druitt informed the inspector that they believed Jenny was hiding something, and the something, had everything to do with a baby.

The police decided to wait until Jenny had her child, before questioning her again.

The two policemen unfortunately were both transferred after that, and the Mavis Beatty case went cold. The two cases were now put in boxes marked "cold case" which was where they stayed for many years.

Chapter 14

Several years on in Springfield

Nothing much had changed in Springfield. The town had a few new shops and cafes and a new basketball stadium and swimming pool / Leisure Centre. New houses dotted the outskirts of the town as more and more people fled the city for a lifestyle change in the country.

Jenny Moore now had two children, both in their teens. Her husband Douglas was still working but spent his weekends drinking at the local pub with his mates, and his evenings just drinking by himself at home. Although he provided for his family to a certain extent, he was not much of a husband. Jenny's parents retired and moved to the South Coast to live. Jenny herself was bored and lazy. She worked part time in the local supermarket as money was tight, with Douglas spending his money on booze and cigarettes. Jenny's two children were a major problem for Jenny. She had absolutely no control over them and considered them to both be nuisances. They were very rebellious. Douglas did not have much to do with them, telling Jenny the children were her problem, and her responsibility and she was too soft on them. He never listened to Jenny when she tried to enlist his help to control them. He did not want to know about them. Douglas was only interested in getting his next packet of cigarettes or his next bottle of beer.

The two children were in high school but not doing very well. Neither of them was very bright. Shane turned to drugs, staying out for nights at a time, snorting cocaine with his no-good mates. Marigold was going through a "Gothic stage", wearing black lipstick and peculiar dark-coloured clothes. She wore rings draping from every part of her body and was always without shoes. She wore fake gold rings on her fingers and an assortment of necklaces around her neck. She and her mother argued all the time. Marigold rarely attended school and when she did was always in trouble when she did attend.

Jenny watched a lot of television during the day, in particular true crime stories.

One of the television channels was running a series of cold cases and the case of the missing baby "Trinity" was due to be filmed. Jenny was horrified. What if they found out the truth. Jenny felt frightened. She needed to keep her mouth well and truly shut if the cops ever came looking for her again. They never came back, in all of the years since she was married.

At the Springfield Police station, officers were preparing to be filmed in relation to the "Trinity" baby case. By then all of the officers originally involved were gone, either having been transferred or retired.

Constable Jennings was curious about the case and decided to look at the old files in preparation for the film series. He was a nice-looking man with a view to being an actor one day. He thought perhaps being on the show might lead to greater things for him as a potential actor.

When he opened the old files, he also found in the next box, documents relating to the unsolved murder case of Mavis Beatty. When he read the last report about Jenny Moore, he wondered if the two cases might be in some way connected. There was a missing baby and then the murder of Mavis Beatty not long after that. Crimes such as these were unusual in a small country town.

The last report on the questioning of Jenny Moore stated the officers intended to return to question Jenny again, but there was no evidence that they ever did. He instantly felt there was something not quite right about Mavis Beatty's death. There were too many unanswered questions.

The last report stated Jenny became visibly upset when questioned about Mavis and a baby, and the interview was terminated because of her emotional state of mind.

Constable Jennings obtained permission from his superior to reinvestigate the case of Mavis Beatty. He found Jenny Moore's address and decided to visit her directly to catch her off guard, in the hope a surprise visit might loosen her tongue.

Trinity Jessica Louise

"Good morning" said Jenny, to the nice-looking young man at her front door. "I am Constable Jennings. May I ask you some questions?" "Sure, why not," answered Jenny as she led him into the lounge room. Jenny played it cool. She could think of no reason why the police would come to her door. Most likely it was to do with her two teenage children she thought. They were always in trouble.

"Do you remember when the police asked you about Mavis Beatty some years back?" he asked. "Oh, poor Mavis, she died didn't she," said Jenny.

Jenny went pale once again. "I only vaguely remember. It was years ago," she replied. "Did Mavis ever have a baby," he asked outright. "No, not one of her own, but she did have one for a short while," said Jenny reluctantly, deciding to tell the police a small part of the story.

"It was years ago; I can't remember when. She was always talking about having a baby and one day she turned up with one, just for a short while. I think she borrowed it," announced Jenny. "How can you "borrow" a baby?" asked Constable Jennings. "Well one day she had it, and the next day she didn't. I thought she may have been babysitting," replied Jenny, nervously.

"Did you ever see the baby?" asked the policeman. "No not really. I only saw it briefly. I think it was a girl because it was dressed in some pink thing and was wrapped in a pink rug. I'm sorry, that's all I know," she added. "I never saw the baby again," she said nervously. "Were Jimmy Willis and Billy Jones involved in any way," asked Constable Jennings. "What do you mean?" asked Jenny anxiously.

"Well, were they around then?" asked the policeman. "Yeah, I guess. They used to drive us in their cars," she added. "You mean the stolen cars?" asked Constable Jennings "I did not know the cars were stolen," lied Jenny. "They never told me the cars were stolen, or I would not have gone with them," she added.

Realizing that Jenny would not tell him anything else of use, Constable Jennings returned to his office to ponder the cases. Were the two cases linked, he wondered. Was Mavis killed because she knew too much. Jenny certainly knew more than she was saying.

Returning to the "Trinity" case he noted that the baby was last seen wearing a pink jumpsuit and was wrapped in a pink shawl. It certainly sounded as if the cases were linked. Jenny had mentioned the baby was wearing pink. Now that Mavis was dead, he was not sure where to turn. He needed more evidence about the Mavis Beatty case. He was almost certain that Billy and Jimmy had some involvement in both cases.

Forensics from a larger town examined the rum bottles found at the scene of Mavis's death. The police in Springfield matched them to the prints of Jimmy Willis and Billy Jones which were on file at the local police station. The bottles were obviously wiped down, however some partial prints remained. The matching prints unfortunately were not enough evidence to connect Billy or Jimmy to Mavis Beatty's death, even though the police felt strongly they killed Mavis to "shut her up". Although the bottles were found near Mavis's body, they could not be sure of exactly when the boys were drinking there. It was well known by everybody; the gold mine site was a favorite meeting place for Jimmy and Billy. The bottles could have been there for days and perhaps even weeks.

Chapter 15

Things were not great for Billy and Jimmy in Springfield. After years of doing community service and suspended sentences, they were now faced with a long period in goal. The men were always out of work, and there was never enough money to buy beer or cigarettes. More recently they started to smoke Marijuana which proved to be expensive. Billy even tried to grow it, until the neighbours dobbed him in, and he and Jimmy spent a few months in gaol for the offense. They hated gaol with a vengeance.

Putting their heads together they tried to figure out how they could get some money quickly. This time they needed big money to cover the mountain of debts they incurred recently. "We need some cash real soon," said Billy. "I know that. The bloody loan shark is on to us. He won't wait for too much longer. He has already threatened to do us harm and I reckon he means it this time," said Jimmy.

"How about we have a go at the bank," said Billy. "You mean rob a bank," replied Jimmy. "Well, why not. They have plenty of cash and we need cash right now," added Billy. The boys decided that it was a very good idea, believing they were smart enough, and brave enough to carry out a bank robbery.

"We need a plan, one which is foolproof," said Jimmy. "Yep, can't let the cops catch us this time," replied Billy. They decided to make a plan on paper, noting all of the details of the building and the surrounds. The men spent days working out their elaborate plan of action. It included smashing locks, stealing a getaway car, and breaking into a safe. They looked on u-tube to find out about safes, thinking that the bank would not have installed a modern safe, so worked on the theory of the safe being old.

They decided the best time to steal from the bank would be on a Saturday afternoon in a week's time when there was a big regional bowls tournament in town. They also figured out how they would need to disarm the security system. They purchased a blow torch to disable the safe and stole some other equipment to smash the security cameras. They went into the bank before the weekend to find out where the security cameras were located, looking outside of the building as well.

The big day arrived and while most people were busy either playing bowls or watching and catering, the men began to carry out what they thought was a brilliant plan of action and foolproof as well. "This time, mate, we can't lose. It's a fantastic plan," said Billy, full of confidence as usual. The first thing they did was to steal a car. The easy part was then done. The car was just sitting in a laneway with the keys in it. They loaded up the car with their equipment and set off for the bank. They looked around but could not see anyone at all, in the vicinity of the bank, or the alley beside it.

They were completely unaware of the extra police presence in the town and especially at the banks. Just as they thought they were safe, having knocked out the security cameras and broken into the safe, they then placed the money from the safe in brown paper bags. Feeling very pleased with themselves the two of them ran towards the alley, where the stolen car was waiting for them. It was there they were picked up by two policemen, who had been secretly watching and following the stolen car in the alley beside the bank. The money was taken from them, and they were escorted to the police station in handcuffs to be charged with robbery of a bank. On the way to the police station, both Billy and Jimmy were laughing and joking, totally unaware of the seriousness of the situation.

When they were planning the robbery, the men agreed to offer the police some small details about the missing baby in order to get a lighter sentence if they were caught. Naturally they would put all of the blame on poor dead Mavis. They believed any information supplied to the police would be enough to get them a lighter sentence.

Both men were assigned duty solicitors. They told them a few small details of the missing child Trinity, asking if they could get a lighter sentence for information. "We will see. There are a number of things to consider," said Mr. Trent, seriously.

Trinity Jessica Louise

Mr. Trent was the solicitor for Jimmy, while Billy was assigned Mr Billings.

"Mr. Trent, I know who took baby Trinity, the one who went missing years ago," said Jimmy, proudly. "How do you know?" asked Mr. Trent. "Well, I saw her with a baby around then," he replied. "Who was the person and where was it?" asked the solicitor. "Oh, in town at one of the shops on the main road, can't remember which one. It was a long time ago," replied Jimmy. "It was mad Mavis Beatty for sure," he announced, thinking that the information would assist his case. Mr Trent said he would pass the information on to the police. Secretly he doubted that the police would believe even one word of it.

When Billy was questioned, he too offered information about baby Trinity. "It was Mavis Beatty you know. She took the screaming kid," he said smugly. "Really," said Mr Billings. "What was the baby doing with Mavis?" he asked. "Well, she must have knicked him," replied Billy. "So, the baby was a boy, was it," he said. "Yep, all dressed in blue too. It even had a blue hat on," he said with a wide grin, thinking that he just gave the solicitor important information. "Where was this?" asked Mr. Billings. "It was at the swimming pool, the one in town," replied Billy. "What do you think Mavis was doing with a small child at a pool?" asked Mr. Billings. "I dunno, probably taking it for a swim," replied Billy with a stupid grin on his face.

The two solicitors told the police what the men had said. "I believe that they do know something about the abduction, and they are trying to blame poor dead Mavis, who can't defend herself," added Mr. Billings. "It is certainly possible the three of them were involved and that somehow Jenny Moore found out about it. I don't think they would have the brains to have planned anything, so whatever happened must have been a spur of the moment thing," said Mr. Billings.

"Well, it will make no difference to the sentencing," said Constable Jennings. "This time those two are going to be locked up for a very long time."

The two idiots were sentenced to a long period of goal when they attended court about three months later. In the meantime, they were held in custody.

They hated the discipline of gaol because having to do as they were told was something that both of them were never used to. They were in the same gaol block, however, did not see each other much, except at mealtimes. The prison guards were warned about the two of them together, which usually meant nothing but trouble, and to try to keep them apart if possible.

Missing his pal Billy, Jimmy palled up with a man named Ron Wilson. Ron was in gaol for beating up his wife more than once. He did not have a very long sentence. He was due to be released in about six months' time. Jimmy and Ron shared a cell and soon became mates, or partners in crime. It turned out that Ron lived in the town of Brinkley which was the next town over from Springfield. The two men found lots to talk about, both being from small country towns so close together.

Jimmy was very vain, and he was also full of his own importance. He and Ron began telling each other stories about their past achievements in the world of crime, each of them trying to outdo the other.

Ron's stories were mostly about his expertise in beating people up, including women. He was very proud of his boxing prowess. Jimmy was proud of his stealing ways, especially in stealing cars. He told Ron about the many ways to steal a car. "Its easy mate, when you know how," said Jimmy, full of pride for his achievements.

One evening after lights out, Jimmy was skiting about his adventures. "You know Ronny, I stole a baby once. I mean I drove the getaway car and dumped the baby at a farmhouse in the next town. There were four of us, but I was the main man," he said. Ronny was suitably impressed. "Wow, you were game," he said. "Yep, it was all over the papers and television. It was years ago." "What happened to the baby?" asked Ronny. "No idea," replied Jimmy. "Could be dead, for all I know," he added.

"The cops never caught us. It was me and Billy and Jenny Moore and stupid mad Mavis. We took the kid from the rodeo at Springfield," Jimmy added. "That must have been a buzz," replied Ronny, once again full of admiration for Jimmy's prowess.

The guards came around then to tell them to be quiet, so the conversation ended.

Chapter 16

Six months later Ronny Wilson was released from prison.

Ronnie Wilson was having an affair with a woman called Gayle, while he was still married to Helen, the wife who was the recipient of the beatings. Helen refused to give Ronny a divorce, which is why he beat her up the second time, because Gayle was putting pressure on him to marry her. The first time he beat her, because she told him she was pregnant, and no way did he want to have some snotty nosed kid to look after. Anyway, she lost the kid, so that was a great result as far as he was concerned. Helen reported the beating to the police and Ronny was charged with assault.

Gayle was waiting for him outside the gaol, in her very old car. She recently dyed her hair blonde and was wearing black tight leather pants and a crop top which showed off too much of her breasts "Oh, it's wonderful to see you my love," she said. "Yep, sure is babe. You are looking really good," said Ronny. "I got us a flat in Springfield," she said. "There were no flats for rent in Brinkley," she added. "Great," replied Ronny, who

Trinity Jessica Louise

didn't care where they lived just as long as she took care of his basic needs.

That night after fish and chips for tea, Ronny talked about his mate Jimmy who was his roommate and friend in prison. "Really cool guy is Jimmy. You know, he told me about the time he stole this kid and dumped it somewhere," Pretty brave, don't you think," he asked Gayle. "Yeah, whatever," replied Gayle, trying to sound enthusiastic.

Gayle was more interested in cuddling up to Ronny on the couch than talking about some crazy prison mate, but she pretended to be interested.

The next day Ronny strolled down to the bottle shop while Gayle went to work at the nursing home where she was a cleaner. Gayle was a very disorganised cleaner, but she was the best of a bad bunch, the nursing home manager thought. Gayle was lazy, but there was not much choice of good cleaners in a small town. That night was her bingo night with her girlfriends. She left Ronny with his beer and watching sport on television. Ronny couldn't care less where she went as long as she was faithful. If she turned out to be unfaithful, he would soon give her the beating of a lifetime.

Gayle met her girlfriends at the bingo hall where they started to enjoy their beer and bingo, in between looking at the numbers, hoping to win a meat parcel, which was the main prize of the night. Lots of gossip was exchanged between the women, as was the norm on bingo nights. "How is Ronny?" asked Judy, one of her friends. "Pretty good. He met some guy called Jimmy in prison who was really cool. Apparently, he stole a baby one day, more than twenty years ago and dumped the kid somewhere. Yeah, it happened somewhere around here I think," she said. "Wow," said Judy.

Sitting at the next table was Julie Jennings, wife of Constable Jennings from the Springfield police. She overheard the conversation. It was not too hard since the women were talking in very loud voices.

The next day, Julie told her husband what she overheard the night before at Bingo. "I knew it," he said. "I just knew that Jimmy and his mate Billy had something more to do with the kidnapping of baby Trinity over twenty years ago." He said, banging his fist on the table.

Constable Jennings reported the conversation to his superior the next day and asked if he could re-interview Jimmy in prison. His superior agreed.

Constable Jennings was granted an interview with Jimmy at the prison. The interview was at ten AM the following day.

Jimmy strolled nonchalantly into the visitor's room in his prison garb and found Constable Jennings already seated on a hard steel prison chair.

"How ya going mate," said Jimmy, as cheeky as ever. "Firstly, I am not your mate," said Constable Jennings. "I want you to tell me about the baby you stole, the story you have been bragging about in here," said Constable Jennings, in a stern voice.

"I thought I told you lot, mad Mavis took that kid," replied Jimmy. "Where did you find the child?" asked

Constable Jennings. "What am I going to get out of it. I want a cell with a window," said Jimmy. "Depends," said the policeman knowing full well that Jimmy was never likely to get a cell with a window.

"Well, mad Mavis pinched the kid from a car at the rodeo," announced Jimmy. "Where did you take the child. I know that Mavis could not drive," added Constable Jennings. "Don't know the place, some farm out of town," replied Jimmy, who was beginning to look rattled. "Out of Springfield?" asked the policeman. "No, out of Brinkley," added Jimmy, who by now was looking just a little bit disturbed. "Where exactly?" asked Constable Jennings. "Sorry mate can't remember so long ago," said Jimmy with a smirk. No way was he going to tell the cops anything else. He wanted to keep them guessing, just for fun.

Constable Jennings left then, going back to his office to have a meeting with the other officers. He did not think that he would get any more information out of Jimmy at that point.

Chapter 17

Jessica spent her first six months overseas touring Europe, visiting Bonn in Germany, the home of Beethoven, the Louvre in Paris and Salzburg, the home of Mozart, like herself a childhood prodigy. She enjoyed the museum dedicated to Mozart, especially the display of his early musical instruments. She absolutely loved Salzburg, so spent several days exploring the charming town with its quaint houses and shops She also visited the home of Johann Sebastion Bach in Germany, being a big fan of his sacred music. She adored the museums and opera houses as well as the lovely scenery in Austria and France, and the Picasso Museum in Barcelona in Spain. She travelled by train, enjoying the beautiful countryside from out of the train windows. Each day was a different experience, sometimes mountain ranges, other days wide shining lakes or beautiful flower gardens. She stayed in bed and breakfast homes or small boutique hotels, meeting some really delightful hosts who welcomed the young Australian woman, travelling alone.

After her backpacking experiences in Europe, Jessica moved first to Scotland where she went on bus tours and stayed at guest houses, and then to England where she then moved to London city to stay for a while. Jessica loved Scotland and the people. She was attracted to old castles and churches. In London she obtained a one-bedroom apartment in Notting Hill and decided to look for a job in a London Pub, not so much for the money, but for the company and the chance to meet new people. She met a lot of Australians during her travels who enjoyed working in English pubs. Although she was happy to be alone to grieve for her parents, she now looked forward to chatting to other people from different countries and various walks of life.

One day she was admiring the flowers and posies in a London flower shop. There was a sign out the front asking for a part time worker. Jessica went into the store and talked to the manager, who agreed to give her the job with a trial period. "I have no experience, but I worked in my parents' large garden. I do know a fair bit about flowers," she said enthusiastically.

Two days a week she worked for the London florist, delivering flowers and sometimes helping to make up flower posies, a job she loved. Her work behind the bar was more exciting, with customers from all over the world frequenting the bar which was named "The Four Black Sheep". Jessica loved the name of the pub and one day decided to go in and introduce herself. The manager said, "We get a lot of Australians in here so it might be good to have an Aussie bar tender. Actually, we are hiring right now if you're interested." He told Jessica that she could start immediately with a week's trial. Jessica was delighted.

Jessica was a bright girl, so it did not take long for her to learn how to pour beer and spirits. She was blessed with a lovely personality, so the customers soon took a liking to the new Australian girl. After her trial week was up, the boss was delighted to employ her on a more permanent basis. Jessica soon made friends with the owner's wife Kathleen and a girl called Wendy who also worked shifts at the pub and was the same age as Jessica.

Sometimes Jessica was required to assist in the kitchen, making up pub meals for the bistro section of the pub. She learnt basic cooking at home with Jess who taught her to make simple dishes like roasts and stews as well as easy desserts like apple crumble and baked custard. Jess never did any fancy cooking, rather she stayed safe with meat and three vegetables. She remembered those days of cooking with her mother with sadness. Sometimes she was required to mop floors and clean glasses. Jessica was happy doing different jobs.

Here at the pub, it was mainly steak pies or fish and chips or hamburgers, and in the mornings eggs and bacon, not too difficult. Jessica got on very well with the chef, who loved her Australian accent. Very soon, Jessica's days became quite busy, leaving little time for grieving or worrying about things happening back home. She hoped her parents would have approved of her current lifestyle. She knew they really wanted her to go to university and to further her studies with the violin and piano, but the time was not right for those things just yet.

Trinity Jessica Louise

The two days a week at the florist shop were not as hectic, however Jessica loved the beautiful flowers which were flown in each day from the Netherlands. The three florists were amazing artists and Jessica learnt a great deal during her time with them. She was often given left- over fresh flowers to take home to her little flat.

Jessica met some great people, mostly around her own age whilst working at the pub. One day she was working the day shift, when a young man came in and ordered a beef steak pie with mushy peas. Jessica started to talk to him in her usual friendly way. He asked her to sit with him for a minute and because it was time for her break, she obliged. He was a very good-looking man with blue-grey eyes and dark blonde hair which curled softly around his ears. His face lit up with a wide-open smile which when he flashed it to Jessica, gave her a lovely feeling inside.

His name was James, and he was originally from the Isle of Skye in Scotland. He was studying medicine at the University in London and was in his final year, so was a few years older than Jessica. Jessica went to a co-ed school back home, so was used to boys staring at her and trying to get her attention, but this man was different. He was much more mature than the boys from school.

"What is your name, beautiful girl?" he asked in his broad Scottish accent. My name is Jessica Louise Bloom," she replied. "Oh, you are an Aussie," he remarked. "Yes, but don't hold it against me," she replied with a laugh. "I won't if you promise not to laugh at my Scottish accent," James replied with a smile which reflected his charming personality.

Most days, when she was on the lunchtime shift, Jessica saw James, and her face would light up at the sight of his lovely gentle face. He always ordered the same meal. One day James asked Jessica if she would like to go to a movie with him at a nearby picture theatre. She was thrilled to bits and spent ages deciding what to wear and how to style her hair. In the end she chose a lovely dark blue dress which lit up her bright blue eyes, with her hair hanging loose around her shoulders in blonde waves. Jessica had never been on a date before and was a little bit nervous. She wondered what people talked about when they were on a date.

Jessica need not have worried. She and James found plenty to talk about. James told Jessica about his childhood, growing up on the Isle of Skye, and Jessica talked about her life on the farm and the distress which she still felt about her parents' deaths. James offered her words of comfort.

That was the first of many dates between James and Jessica. They talked about everything, both being very comfortable in each other's company. James needed to study a lot and carry out work placements, but they still managed to see each other once or twice a week. Jesssica did not need to concern herself about what to talk about. After a few months they knew everything, possible there was to know about each other.

On weekends if James was not working, they would take a picnic to one or other of London's beautiful parks, watching the ducks on the small lakes and just relaxing on their tartan rugs.

Jessica did not have any relationships with boys or men on which to base her knowledge, but she was sure that her feelings for James could be considered romantic and was pretty sure he felt the same way. Indeed, by his actions and conversations he certainly showed his keen interest in her.

After six months living in London, Jessica and James attended a concert one night. It was a night of beautiful music, with much loved classical pieces from different composers, leading Jessica to think of her own experiences with the piano and violin. She told James about having learnt to play the violin at six years of age, and how she wanted to study music, further on in the future.

Following the concert Jessica invited James up to her apartment and before they knew it, they were kissing and ending up in her large bed together making love. Jessica's parents did not talk to her much about relationships with the opposite sex. Perhaps they wanted to wait until she was older, she thought. It was Jessica's first experience of love making, and James was gentle and loving, as she knew he would be. In the morning neither of them felt any regrets. James told Jessica that he loved her and always would. "I love you too, James," she replied.

Jessica and James continued seeing each other for the next few months. James owned a motorcycle with a sidecar, so many trips were taken to the seaside and local parks whenever James had time. His studies in medicine were almost completed and he was now starting to think about where he would go next, always hoping Jessica would wish to go with him. "I think I will go to a country hospital next year. Would you like living in the country again?" asked James. "Yes, I would love it," replied Jessica.

Jessica and James began to talk about marriage. "Do you want children, James?" asked Jessica. "Yes, I definitely do. Especially with you, my dearest love, and I don't want to wait too long either," he replied happily. "What about you, Jessica. Do you see a family in your future with me," "Definitely," said Jessica with enthusiasm. They kissed and went home to their respective houses, secure in their love for each other. Jessica was starting to feel alive again, after the trauma of her parents' deaths.

One evening when she was working a late shift at the bar, Jessica looked up to see James' best friend, Peter come into the pub with a serious look on his face. Jessica took one look at Peter's face, and instantly knew it meant something bad, and the something bad concerned James she immediately thought. "Peter what is wrong?" asked Jessica. "Jessica, I don't know how to tell you. I'm so, so sorry. There has been an accident," he said, quietly "Is it James?" she asked, shaking all over. "Yes, it is. I'm afraid he was killed in an accident on his motorbike," Peter announced with tears in his eyes. Jessica looked at Peter in stunned silence. "Are you sure it is James?" she asked Peter. "There is no doubt. I identified him," he replied.

Jessica collapsed onto the floor. "No, no, it can't be true," she cried. Suddenly the vision of her parents' deaths came back to her. It was the same awful nightmare, returning to haunt her. Jessica did not know what to do or where to go. Her work colleagues surrounded her with love and comfort. They wrapped her in a warm blanket and gave her hot drinks as she dealt with the immediate shock. Kathleen and Wendy hugged her tightly. Everyone at the pub knew James and all of them loved him. They felt terribly sorry for Jessica.

One of the workers from the pub, escorted Jessica home in his car and took her upstairs to her bedroom. They were all so kind to her, but nothing would ease her pain or could bring James back.

Jessica returned home to her little flat feeling terribly sad, lost and alone, the place where she and James first declared their love for each other. She could not believe once again, someone she loved so dearly was now dead. What was wrong with her, to make people she loved leave her so alone and afraid. She cried into the night and woke in the morning with a bad headache and an even deeper pain in her heart. She could hardly believe her beloved James, like her parents, was gone. It did not seem fair, Jessica thought.

James' body was returned to his Scottish home on the Isle of Skye and there was a small memorial service held at the hospital where he was working until his death. He was a very popular young man, destined for great things, dying so tragically and so young. Jessica attended the service in a plain black dress which she borrowed from a workmate and covered her head with a small black hat and veil to cover her eyes now full of tears. She returned to her little flat still crying nonstop.

Once again, Jessica was faced with indecision as she tried to find a way through her grief. Working helped a bit but was not the answer. She still needed to return to her lonely little flat at night. Her new friends from the florist shop and the pub tried their best to help her through the dreadful time. Nothing seemed to lesson her grief.

She started to think about home. It would not be the same without her parents, but Jessica knew she needed to start over once again. She thought starting over might be easier in Australia, knowing it would not be without problems, in whatever place she chose. Jessica felt she now was faced with only one choice. She needed to go home, back to the country where she was born.

Chapter 18

Jessica stayed on in London for another month to sort out her flat and give notice to her two employers who were sorry to lose the lovely young Australian girl, but completely understood her reason for needing to go home. Her friends held a farewell party for her at the pub. She was sad to say goodbye to them, but she felt sure she needed to leave and start again.

It was about eighteen months since she set out from her country to travel across to the other side of the world. She was now over twenty years old but felt older, due to the experiences she endured.

Once again, she boarded a large plane to return home, still carrying her backpack which served her well. The trip was long and boring. Jessica tried to sleep, but her mind kept returning to her loss. Would she ever get over it, she wondered. She tried to watch the movies on the plane or to read a book but could not concentrate.

On her return to Sydney, Jessica checked into a nice hotel near Bondi beach, so she could try to work out what she should do now. Jessica always wanted to go to the beach as a child, but her parents usually made up an excuse as to why they could not go. She walked on the beach each evening collecting shells and watching people swimming in the sea and walking their dogs. She felt a sense of calm settle upon her, as she saw people out and about, enjoying their lives. Perhaps she too could have a future she thought, as she watched families playing happily together. She was still young enough to have a future and maybe one day to have a child of her own.

Jessica debated where to live next. She thought of returning to the country town in which she grew up, but the memories of the farm and her hometown made her feel sad, so she felt a change of scenery was needed in order for her to move on.

It was always Jessica's wish to take her music studies further, and so she made the decision to apply to the Sydney Conservatorium of Music, the music school of Sydney University in order to further her studies of the violin, her preferred instrument. She deferred her studies from the Sydney University, prior to going overseas, so it was not too difficult to resume her studies there.

Her violin was stored with other items in a storage unit in Sydney, so she went to get it in order to do some practice before she received an interview, that was if she even got as far as an interview. She also contacted her old music teacher, Adam and asked him for a reference which he was happy to supply.

A few weeks later, Jessica was called in for an interview.

Trinity Jessica Louise

Taking her mother's antique violin and her reference and wearing her favourite blue dress with her mother's string of pearls around her neck, Jessica set off nervously for her audition at the "Con". She felt calm and confident as she approached the lovely old white building which was founded in 1915 and became iconic in Australia. Jessica knew that the "Con" research advances music across all of its sub-disciplines through artistic exploration, music scholarship and fieldwork She believed it was the perfect place for her to study.

There were three people conducting the interview as well as herself in the room. There were two women and one man. They asked her to sit and tell them about herself. When she said she had been playing the violin since she was six, they raised their eyebrows and started to pay more attention.

Jessica decided to play her favourite violin concerti by Antonio Vivaldi, entitled "The Four Seasons", composed around 1720, but still a popular choice today.

Jessica was comfortable with her chosen piece and now relaxed after the three people showed her, they were human after all, through pleasant conversations with her. She played with all of the skill she remembered so well, and although a little nervous managed to illicit a great response from the three judges, who clapped enthusiastically after her performance.

Following her audition Jessica returned to the small boutique hotel, and back in her room pondered her next steps. She decided she could not live in the hotel forever. It was not a question of money, but rather she felt like she needed some company now, after having a joyful time with James and before then with her parents. She did not think she was meant to live alone forever. She thought of getting a flat as she did in London, but decided she wanted a bit more of a life with other people.

Jessica decided to find a share house and commenced reading the advertisements in the daily newspaper. Most of the advertisements were students looking to share, however Jessica felt, being a bit older she might not fit in, especially if they wanted to party or play loud modern music.

Chapter 19

Reading the classifieds in the daily newspaper one night, Jessica found an advertisement for a share house which seemed to suit her needs. It said;

"Wanted – Young woman to share house with elderly lady.

Northern beaches area.

Assistance required with meal preparation and shopping.

Own room and bathroom.

Use of lounge and television.

Quiet respectable area.

Must be quiet and neat.

No smoking or drinking permitted."

Jessica liked the sound of the advertisement, so decided to visit the house at the address shown. It was only a short bus ride to the house. She dressed in a patterned skirt and white blouse. The house was old and beautiful. It was obviously well cared for in the past, situated in a beautiful area of Sydney with lots of old English trees having been planted long ago in some of the streets in the suburbs.

She knocked on the door and waited for a while, until she heard footsteps approaching slowly. The door opened and a woman stood there looking startled and cross. She appeared to be about sixty or more and she was surrounded by a mop of wild white hair around her face. "Well, what do you want, missy?" she asked Jessica. "What are you selling?" she asked impatiently.

Jessica thought the woman looked a bit crazy and almost turned and ran out of the gate. "I am here about the share house," replied Jessica quietly. "Oh that. I have forgotten that I placed the advertisement. Well, I have changed my mind," she said in an unfriendly tone. "But why?" asked Jessica. "I decided I don't want anybody nosey," she replied. "Well, I am not nosey," said Jessica as she turned to leave. "Come back here girl. Let me take a good look at you," said the woman in a nicer tone this time.

Jessica was not sure how to react to the woman. She did not know whether to go or stay. The woman said, "All right, you can come in now." So Jessica followed her into the house. They entered a beautiful foyer decorated with early Australian paintings and Persian rugs on the polished floor. There was a large, elegant chandelier on the ceiling. The woman led her into a big lounge room with leather chairs and told her to sit down which she did, still unsure if the woman was crazy or just plain cranky. Perhaps she was in pain, thought Jessica who was a kind girl.

"Well missy, tell me about yourself," the woman said, a bit more friendly this time. Jessica told her a bit about herself and gave her all relevant information like age, name and family history. In return the woman told Jessica her name which was Jane Smithers, and said she needed a bit of help around the house, since she was not long out of hospital, after breaking her hip and having a full hip replacement. "I'm sure I can be of help. I know how to cook and shop, and I am neat and tidy. I don't have any bad habits like smoking, nor do I go out partying," said Jessica.

"Well, you look respectable enough," said Jane. "I suppose we can give it a try. I am sorry I snapped at you. My hips are very painful today," she added. "I know a lot of pain can be upsetting," answered Jessica as she remembered her mother complaining about pain from arthritis. "My mother suffered from arthritis, so I know how pain can make you feel dreadful at times," she added sympathetically. Jane was pleased to know Jessica was compassionate.

They arranged for Jessica to move in a couple of days' time. Jessica went back to her hotel and wondered what on earth she got herself into. She decided if Jane was too crazy, or the place did not suit then she could always leave. At least she knew the house was beautiful, and the surrounding area was nice too.

Chapter 20

Jane Smithers was normally a spritely woman in her late sixties. She kept up with daily news and politics and read a lot of books in different genres, although mysteries were her favourite. She grew up in a Sydney church orphanage, after being dumped on church steps when she was a tiny baby by her mother who could not afford to feed her. Her mother already gave birth to three other children. Her mother attached a note to her clothing which said "Please take care of my little girl. I cannot provide for the baby." She also left a small silver locket. Although Jane was fed and clothed at the orphanage, it was a busy place where the staff cared for a large number of children, leaving very little time for mothering or storytelling.

Jane was never lucky enough to have been chosen for adoption, so remained at the place until she was eighteen. At the orphanage Jane led a simple life, working with the nuns to do cooking, and caring for the younger children. Although she just turned eighteen, she was very naive and unaware of the world outside of the orphanage or the dangers which could befall a young unworldly woman.

It was an Anglican orphanage run by Church of England nuns, so Jane was used to attending daily prayers and weekly services at the church. Jane also worked in the kitchen helping with meal preparation and doing mountains of dishes. She did not like doing dishes. They seemed to be a never-ending nightmare. She learned a lot about cleaning as well, not that she enjoyed it one bit, but she was very good at it, liking everything to be clean and tidy.

Just before she turned eighteen, Jane was sent to Reverent Charles's office to do some cleaning. She often cleaned rooms at the orphanage, being well known for her attention to detail in her cleaning routine. Jane began to scrub the black and white tiles on the office floor, and was bending down to kneel on the floor, when Reverent Charles, the minister came up behind her and grabbed her by the breasts. He then forced himself on Jane who did not know what was happening to her and was very frightened. When he finished assaulting her, he stood up to his full height which was over six feet two and said nastily "If you tell anyone about this, I will make sure that everyone here knows that you're not a nice girl, and you seduced me and led me on." "You will be shunned, and no-one will ever employ you," he added in a tone full of scorn.

Jane was horrified. She had no experience of men or sex. She picked herself up from the floor where he threw her, with her hair in a tousled mess, and clothes disheveled.

Her immediate reaction was to run. There was no-one who could help her or whom she felt that she could trust. She did not think anyone would believe her, especially when Reverent Charles was considered to be such an upstanding, honourable man. She felt certain the nuns would think she made up the story to get attention.

Her first instinct was to run away. She could think of nothing else to do, so she ran, taking with her, only a small bag of possessions. She owned one good dress which she wore on Sundays, two books and a silver locket which her mother had left with her.

It was evening when she left, with absolutely no idea of where she was going or to how she could get there. She lived a very sheltered life in the orphanage.

Jane decided to run towards the light which happened to be in the Sydney area of King's Cross, a notorious crime area of Sydney. It was also known as a place where ladies of the night conducted their business, not that Jane knew anything about those things. An older girl saw her standing alone on a corner and said, "You better not stand there, it's dangerous and you may be mistaken for a hooker."

"What's a hooker?" Jane asked the other girl. She did not reply, thinking that it was too long an explanation which could wait. Jane moved to the footpath and the other girl asked her if she was okay. Jane shook her head and started to cry. Julie, the older girl took her hand and led her upstairs to her one room flat above a convenience store. "Come with me. It's not safe for you here," said Julie, taking Jessica by the hand. "Are you hungry?"

asked Julie. "I can make some soup and toast," she added. Jane nodded. She suddenly felt hungry. After they finished eating, Julie said, "Let's leave everything until morning and then you can tell me what the problem is."

Jane slept on a mattress on the floor beside her new friend whose name was Julie Evans. Jane woke up to find the sun already up and Julie making coffee. Jane told her what took place at the orphanage. "I am so sorry. That is simply awful," said Julie to the young woman. Julie was not much older than Jane but was years ahead of her in knowledge of the ways of the world.

The owner of the convenience store was looking for an assistant, so Julie took Jane to meet him. He was a nice man to work for. Jane did not have any experience but was a quick learner and was also very honest and tidy, so the owner kept her on after the first trial week.

Jane was working at the store for two months, when one day a young man came in and started chatting to Jane, who was now looking more attractive in Julie's borrowed clothes. Before long the young man whose name was John Smithers and Jane were the best of friends. Jane and John went to the movies together, took long walks in the park and visited the library together. They soon became close friends.

John was in the army and was about to go overseas to war, so he asked Jane to marry him after just having known her for only a short time. She was not really sure about it, but he was very keen, so they were married in a registry office at the local courthouse, just a few days before he was shipped out. "I really want to marry you before I go, just in case anything happens to me while I am serving my country," he said in a serious tone. Jane understood the urgency. Many other couples married for the same reason.

Jane and John went to a hotel at the blue mountains for a short honeymoon of just six days. Soon it was time for John to go to face the war. Jane stood with all of the other wives and girlfriends as they waved goodbye to their loved ones heading overseas.

After a few months of letter writing and with a long distance between them, Jane almost felt as if she was not married. She discovered when her breasts were sore and her weight went up, she was pregnant. She told Julie who said, "Do you want this baby Jane?" At first, she was dismayed, but then she felt happy. At least she would not feel lonely again. She was most unwell during the first trimester but managed to hold down her job in spite of everything. Jane wrote to John to tell him the happy news which she hoped would cheer him up as he fought for his country in war.

Jane received news of her husband's death by telegram when she was just over three months pregnant. What on earth am I going to do now, she said to herself. Jane hoped he received her letter before he died. "I am pregnant with no husband to look after me," she told Julie, miserably.

One evening she felt awful cramps in her tummy as the baby came away. She did not go to the hospital. Julie took care of her, placing hot towels on her tummy to

Trinity Jessica Louise

help with the pain. Afterwards she forced her to eat and exercise after the baby aborted. Jane cried for a long while after she lost the baby, her only reminder of her short marriage to John. John would have been so happy to have become a father. Jane was feeling depressed and unwell after the loss of her baby and John's death.

Jane received a letter two months later from a legal firm representing John Smithers, her husband. It seemed her husband was from a very wealthy family. His father, Malcolm Smithers, died a few weeks before John. John inherited his father's large estate which as his wife, now belonged to Jane. John was an only child. Jane was stunned to hear the news which made her a very wealthy widow. Instead of just struggling to get by each week, she now received enough money on which to live for the rest of her life.

Jane never married again and purchased her current home many years ago. She worked for a number of charities, mostly concerning children and was a generous benefactor to hospitals and orphanages around the country.

Jane never forgot Julie or her kindness to her during a really bad time in her life. She purchased a little house for her, where Julie now lived with her husband and two children. Julie was happy to give up her miserable life as a "lady of the night" and remained a long-term close friend of Jane.

Chapter 21

Moving day arrived quickly, as Jessica left the Hotel and prepared to join Jane at her lovely old house. She did not have many clothes or large items, just her violin, her most precious possession. Her worldly goods were contained in a small suitcase. She still stored a few items in her storage unit, but decided to wait before collecting them, just in case the agreement with Jane did not work out.

A receptionist from the conservatorium of music administration phoned Jessica just before she left the hotel to say they were pleased to offer her a place to study the violin at their school. Jessica was over the moon with joy. It was the nicest thing to happen to her in a long while. It was just as well they phoned her at the hotel, because she was yet to inform them of her new address.

Jessica entered the gate leading up to Jane's home with mixed feelings. In a hurry, she forgot to tell Jane about her music aspirations, so was not sure how her new landlady would take it. Not everyone would enjoy the violin as much as Jessica did.

Jane came to the door and seemed much more pleasant that she first appeared at their last meeting. She took Jessica into a lovely light filled room, charmingly decorated in colours of green and pink. It was a very feminine room. Lace curtains adorned the windows and colourful paintings lined the walls. "What a beautiful room this is," she said. Jane was pleased.

On the way downstairs, Jessica noticed a large baby grand piano on the landing. She thought now might be a good time to discuss with Jane her music studies.

"Jane, I have something to ask you, which you may decide is a problem for me living here," said Jessica. "Are you going to tell me that you smoke pot and take illegal drugs?" asked Jane. "No, nothing illegal at all. It's just that I am studying music at the conservatorium of music, actually the violin and I also play the piano, so I will need to practice," replied Jessica.

"Why that is wonderful," said Jane. "I absolutely love classical music and will welcome the sound of it in my home. I used to play the piano once, but arthritis has put a stop to all piano playing now," she added. "You may use the piano whenever you wish. I keep it well tuned all the time." Jane was thrilled to be able to have her home filled with music once again.

Jessica took her violin and few possessions into her nice new room, feeling very comfortable with the arrangements. It did not take her long to unpack. She was happy to have such a large room with the double bed adorned a with a homemade quilt. There were two bedside tables and a desk in the room as well. She found

Jane and organised to do some grocery shopping for her, in order to make dinner for the evening. Jane said she preferred simple meals as Jessica's parents did, making things easier for Jessica.

Jessica walked to the shops, heading first to the supermarket for meat and groceries and then to the green grocers for fresh fruit and vegetables. When she arrived home, she cooked lamb chops with potatoes and beans for the main meal, then baked a simple rice pudding for dessert. "That was a lovely meal," said Jane with a smile. Jessica was pleased such a simple dish could make Jane happy. She was probably sick and tired of hospital food.

Jessica decided Jane was really soft underneath and probably her bark was worse than her bite as the saying went.

Jessica started her new studies the following week and after a few days was settled into a routine with school, cooking, and shopping for Jane. There was a cleaner who came in three days a week, doing all the washing and vacuuming, leaving Jessica time to practice her violin and piano. Jane enjoyed hearing Jessica play the classical music.

Jessica found the study of the composers a delight, especially since she visited so many of their ancient places of birth while on her travels through Europe. While history was a part of her studies, she especially enjoyed the practical side of her studies, where she was the most outstanding in her group.

Chapter 22

Jessica was never ill. One day she felt nauseous and a bit tired. She put it down to something she ate at the university campus canteen. After a couple of weeks, the nausea seemed to settle down, but she still felt tired. "I must slow down." She told herself, and immediately started to reduce her violin practice hours by an hour a day.

Jane became concerned about her because she appeared to have lost some weight. She encouraged Jessica to go to visit her own doctor who looked after Jane for many years and was a kindly soul. Jessica was reluctant to go, still insisting there was nothing wrong with her. In the end she became sick of Jane fussing over her and decided to go see the doctor to please Jane, and to put her mind at rest. "I am only going to please you Jane," she announced.

Old Dr. Neal welcomed Jessica, telling her how pleased he was that she was now caring for Jane. "She looks so much better these days and has put on weight. It must be your good cooking," he said with a smile. "Now, what is going on with you my dear," he asked.

Jessica replied "Oh, Jane is just fussing a bit. She wanted me to come. There is nothing wrong with me, I am certain. I never get sick," she answered.

Dr. Neal ordered blood tests and examined Jessica thoroughly. "My dear, I won't say for certain until I get the test results back, but I do believe you are pregnant," he said.

"Pregnant" replied Jessica with a look of dismay on her face. "Yes, I think about three months," he said. "I was not expecting to hear I might be pregnant," said Jessica looking dismayed.

Jessica thought back to the last time she and James made love. It was about three months ago she thought. She told Dr. Neal about James and how they loved each other and about the terrible accident in London which killed him. "We planned to marry, you know," said Jesssica, not wanting Dr. Neal to think she slept around with different men.

"So, do you want to keep this baby?" he asked. "Just now I am still in shock, so I need to think about it," she answered. "Well don't think about it for too long. You are already over three months gone," he replied. "I don't have any financial worries, and I would really love to have James' baby," replied Jessica.

He went on to tell her how difficult it might be to be a single mother, and perhaps she needed to think about her studies and the time and energy they took, so she went home with a lot of things to think about.

Trinity Jessica Louise

When she arrived home, Jane was waiting to talk to her. She simply said she was having some blood tests done and went to her room to think.

Jessic knew she could talk to Jane about anything as they had become good friends over the past weeks, and she trusted Jane. Just now she needed to work through what Dr. Neal informed her of, and to try to figure out what was the best way to handle the situation she now found herself in.

Jessica was restless during the night, trying to decide what to do. She recognised the problems possibly facing her in the future if she did decide to keep the baby, however she also thought how the child would always remind her of James, and how much he loved her.

In the end she decided to discuss the matter with Jane. Jane was older and wiser with, more life experiences than Jessica who by now valued her opinion.

Jessica sat down after dinner one evening to talk to Jane about her dilemma. She told her how much she loved James and how she did not feel right about aborting his baby.

"Well Jessica, I was pregnant once, many years ago. My new husband went to the war and never came home. We were only married a short time. I was three months pregnant when he was killed in overseas. I really wanted to have his baby, however I miscarried after hearing of John's death, much to my disappointment and still today I wish the child was alive so I could have a permanent memory of our love. Of course, you should do what you want but if it was me, I would keep the baby," she added.

"I do have money of my own Jane, but can I still live with you here if I have a baby?" Jessica asked. "Of course you can my dear," replied Jane. "I will love a little baby. It will remind me of the little one I lost," she added.

And so, it was decided that Jessica would have the baby and continue to live with Jane. The timing was perfect as far as university went because Jessica was due to give birth to her child during the long summer break. She didn't want to miss any of her university sessions.

In the evenings Jane and Jessica spent time together, with Jessica playing the piano, or both of them playing cards or just simply reminiscing. Since the reveal of Jessica's pregnancy, both ladies took up knitting and sewing to make baby clothes for the coming infant. Jane was extremely fast on her sewing machine, turning out nighties and dresses each week.

Jessica continued to be fit and healthy for the first few months. She coped very well with her studies, still enjoying her practical lessons with her violin.

When Jessica reached her third semester, she woke up one day with an extremely sore throat. She membered having a few colds as a child, but nothing as bad as this. She was unusually tired and was hardly able to walk. She could barely swallow and was nauseous. After a while her breathing became laboured, and she could hardly speak. Jane decided to phone Dr. Neal who was able to make a house call straight away. After he examined Jessica, he raced to the phone, to call an ambulance. It arrived ten minutes later and transported the very sick young woman to hospital. "What do you think it is, Dr. Neal?" asked

Jane anxiously. "I can't be sure, but it looks like Diphtheria to me," he said. "Diphtheria," said Jane, in horror. "I thought the disease was eradicated in Australia," she exclaimed. "So did I," he added, solemnly. "I have only ever seen two cases in my entire working life," he said.

At the hospital, Jessica was placed in a private isolation ward due to the suspicion of diphtheria which is a nasty disease transmitted from person to person She was immediately given antibiotics and anti-toxins. She was not allowed any visitors. The hours went by with Jessica being nursed by masked and gowned registered nurses. She needed help with her breathing. Due to her pregnancy, the doctors were very concerned. After the second day, Jessica seemed to improve a little. The antibiotics appeared to be working and her temperature came down. Dr. Neal reported the update to Jane who was desperately worried.

By day three, Jessica's condition was changed from critical to serious and the medical staff breathed a sigh of relief. She was still considered to be contagious. On day five Jane was allowed to visit but only with a mask in place. "My girl, you did give us all a terrible fright," said Jane. "I am sorry to have worried you Jane, "she said, softly. "It is not your fault. You did not get sick on purpose," Jane added.

Chapter 23

The sore throat continued on for some days, but the baby seemed to be doing well, which was the biggest worry for Jessica. She was looking forward to having James' baby so much and did not want to lose it now. Jane took her some fresh clothes, and she was permitted to get out of bed to take a walk around the hospital garden.

The specialist who cared for Jessica, visited her one evening during his evening rounds. He asked her if she knew about what immunisations she was given as a child. "I believe you may have been given some earlier immunisations but not all of the required boosters," he added. "The fact that you responded so well to treatment leads us to think you may have received some immunity but not totally." "I can't ever recall ever having any booster shots for anything," said Jessica, a bit alarmed.

Jessica thought back to what the doctor told her about the community nurse not receiving any documents from her parents in relation to her childhood immunisations and was intrigued as to why her mother did not produce them, when asked. Perhaps because I never did have them,

Trinity Jessica Louise

she thought. She certainly could not remember ever having injections of any kind whilst growing up.

When she arrived home, during a conversation with Jane, she told her she did not believe her mother took her to have any childhood immunisations. Certainly, she never remembered having any booster shots, during her primary or high school years. "Perhaps you should see Dr. Neal and ask about it," replied Jane.

When she next saw Dr. Neal, she asked him why her parents may have chosen not to take her to be immunised. "Rarely, parents do not feel the need or have strong feelings about it. The important thing is that we can do all of the booster shots now. We might never know why your parents did not keep up to date with your immunisations. It is very strange in this day and age for people to not give their children immunisations," he said.

Jessica could think of no reason why her parents would have a negative attitude towards immunisations. They were pretty average people, not people who held strong objections to anything really. They valued their privacy which was not necessarily a bad thing, she thought.

Jessica phoned Roslyn Myer to ask about her parents' beliefs. Roslyn was very upset to hear about Jessica's recent stay in hospital, but she was delighted to hear about the baby, and told Jessica how she would love to visit her when the baby arrived. "I don't think they would have any feelings about immunisations one way or another. They probably just didn't ever get around to it," she added. "I can't ever remember having any booster shots growing up," said Jessica. "Well, that is really odd," Roslyn replied.

Jessica was left with no answers once again. She wished that she knew more about her parents' life when they were first married. They never talked about her birth or her mother's pregnancy. There was some mystery in her parents' marriage, something which they never talked about, and Jessica was determined to find out about it. She needed to find out more of their story for her own piece of mind.

Following her illness and stay in hospital, Jessica continued to improve and was starting to look forward to becoming a mother. She felt she was having a big baby. It was certainly one who moved around a lot.

Before long, she was eight months pregnant. Jane insisted on purchasing a baby cradle, pram, bath and highchair for the new baby. Jessica and Jane went on a wonderful shopping spree, buying nappies and baby items for the new arrival. The spare bedroom was turned into a nursery and painted out in a soft yellow colour, with new curtains made in yellow gingham check. Jessica made the curtains using Jane's sewing machine. The chest of drawers in the room was full to the brim with nighties, singlets and day wear in different sizes.

Jessica completed her first year of university getting the top marks out of all the students. She was surprised because she missed a lot of classes when she was ill.

Chapter 24

Meanwhile back in the town of Brinkley where Jessica grew up, her new lawyer Greg Lawson was cleaning out his father's private papers after he recently died. Looking through the many boxes of old documents, Greg found some rather strange items. There were all sorts of passports and birth certificates in various names accompanied by notes attached to them. There were also IOU notes made out to various people and a small amount of cash.

The IOU's turned out to belong to some of his father's friends, and a few named various known local loan sharks and bookmakers. He wondered why his father would have made dealings with bookmakers, and why he kept so many passports in different names. Greg asked his mother discreetly one day. "All I know is, I often heard people coming and going at night, sometimes very late. I always wondered what it was about, but your dad just told me it was business and nothing to do with me. I thought it was strange to do business late at night, but I never questioned him. I just thought the callers were people who could not get to the office during the day, such as farmers or truck drivers," she added.

Greg found a piece of paper with the names Jess and Will Bloom, followed by their address and two words "birth certificate" written beside it. What was it all about, he wondered. Why would he have such a strange piece of paper in his documents with nothing else to interpret it. He started to believe his father must have been dealing in some shady business. He decided to sleep on it and try to find out more about his father, not from his mother because she seemed in the dark as well, and he did not want her to worry, as her health was not good.

Greg started to ask around some of his dad's former friends to see if he could find out a bit more about his father's business. Most of his father's friends were very tight lipped, not wanting to get involved, however one friend named Evan McDonald told Greg he believed old Mr. Lawson was heavily in debt and would have done anything to get out of it. He said, "Your dad was a heavy gambler, Greg. He lost thousands by betting on the horses and the trots as well, and I know that his bookmakers were always chasing him. His friends all tried to help him by getting him into gamblers anonymous, but he could not keep it up," "Do you think he would do anything illegal, like forging passports or birth certificates?" asked Greg. "Yes, I think he may have been desperate enough in the end," replied Evan.

Greg found a local bookmaker who knew his dad. "What can you tell me about my dad. Did you ever have any dealings with him?" asked Greg. "Well, he loved to play the horses and the trots and was always owing me money, so I think he would have tried anything to get out of trouble," said the bookmaker. "I did hear on the grapevine he was doing a few dodgy things to make money," he added. "Do you mean like fake passports and birth certificates?" asked Greg. "Yes, things like that," replied the bookmaker. "I don't like to speak ill of the dead, but your father often experienced money problems due to his gambling," he added.

Greg went away with a changed view of his father. He loved his dad, but he also knew gamblers would do anything if they were desperate enough. He was never aware of his dad having money problems. He was away at university, paid for by his father and always thought that his parents were well off. He did not have any idea of his father's true background. He kept his gambling and money troubles a secret from most people. Greg was glad his mother never found out about his father's gambling and money problems.

Greg thought of the conversation which occurred some time ago with the beautiful girl Jessica Bloom, whose parents died in an accident. He remembered her trying to find out some more of her family background, especially a birth certificate.

He found her address from her file as he still managed some of her investments and now handled the lease of the farm which was ongoing.

One day he phoned her and told her what he found in some papers among his father's belongings, including the piece of paper with "birth certificate" written on it besides her parents' name. "I believe my father was making up fake passports and dodgy birth certificates to pay off his gambling debts," Greg said. "I have talked to one of his friends and his bookmaker, and it seems as if he was in a lot of financial trouble," he added.

Jessica was stunned. "So, what you are thinking, Greg, is that my parents forged a fake birth certificate, made up for me by your father," "Yes, Jessica, that is exactly what I believe," said Greg seriously. "Does that mean I may have been adopted?" she asked. "It is certainly very possible," he added. "Have you ever thought of doing a DNA test. Getting a DNA test might give you some clarity," said Greg, wanting to help the young woman if he could.

Jessica told him it was not something she ever would have thought to have done, but she did have a lot of questions and no answers.

Jessica told Jane about the conversation. Jane was intrigued. She remembered what Jessica confided to her about the lack of photographs, having not received any immunisations, and she started to think the lawyer was possibly right. She also remembered how Jessica's parents never allowed her to stay after Sunday school or Pony club. Nor would they allow her to go the shops with her friends or have anyone stay over for the night.

"How can I get DNA when my parents are dead?" she asked Jane. "Well do you have any of their possessions which might assist?" said Jane, trying to be helpful as usual.

I do have my mother's hairbrush set, but I am not sure if there is any hair left in it," she said. "Well, it's worth a try. You need to have hair follicles or roots to be certain, "said Jane seriously.

Jessica took a trip to the storage unit and brought home the brush and comb set, as well as a couple of other boxes of items. "Are you sure you want to do this?" asked Jane. "It might become distressing for you," she added.

"Yes, I do need to know, one way or another," replied Jessica.

She found lots of hair in the comb and the brush, which she removed and placed in a plastic folder, then sent off an application for a full DNA test for the contents as well as her own DNA sample. She was told that it would be several weeks before she would know anything. Jessica prayed that there would be enough hair roots for the DNA testing to be carried out.

Jessica waited and waited for the results of the DNA testing. She went out to the mailbox every day to see if the letter was there.

Seven weeks later, Jessica received the mail she was waiting for. Jane sat beside her on the couch as she opened the large letter. "I am praying I can get some answers now," remarked Jessica.

There was no doubt. The DNA from her mothers' hair and from herself did not match. Jessica could hardly believe it. The mother she loved so much, was not her biological mother. It seemed that she was most probably adopted as a baby, but from where and from whom. Her questions remained once again unanswered. Jessica was stunned. Even though she wondered if she was adopted, she was not prepared for the shock she got, to find out it was actually true.

"I wonder if my father was really my father, or was I adopted from somewhere else," Jessica asked Jane. "It's hard to say," replied Jane, thoughtfully. "Most probably you were adopted from an unmarried mother, or through an adoption agency. From what you have told me about your parents, it does not seem likely that your father would have ever even have thought about an affair. Your parents loved each other." Jane added. "Yes, that is true," Jessica agreed. She could never imagine her father having an affair and then Jess accepting another woman's child.

Chapter 25

Jessica was now a few days overdue with her baby. She tried walking around the block, several times in fact, but nothing happened. She almost took castor oil, however Jane talked her out of it. Jessica was sick of feeling uncomfortable especially at night, when she was trying to sleep.

At last, when she was a week overdue, during the night, after a busy day, Jessica started to have some pains in her front and back. She did not wake Jane until the morning, when her pains became more frequent and more intense. She managed to breathe through the contractions as they became closer. When her water broke shortly afterwards, Jane ordered a taxi, and they took off in haste to the Royal North Shore hospital arriving at about eight o'clock in the morning.

Jessica was taken straight to the labour ward, followed by Jane who told them she was Jessica's mother, so she was allowed in. At about ten AM, the doctor arrived just in time to deliver Jessica's baby. Jane stayed and held her hand, urging her on, as a lovely blue-eyed girl with a tiny bit of fair hair came into the world. She was a big, beautiful baby whom Jessica thought was an absolute miracle. Jane said, "She looks exactly like you Jessica." The baby weighed eight pounds, eight ounces. Jane was mesmerised by the sheer beauty of the child. She knew that Jessica was beautiful and from what Jessica told her, believed James was a handsome man, so she was not surprised.

Jessica coped well with feeding her new daughter so was allowed to return home on the third day. Jane was excited and organised everything ready for their arrival.

After the baby was fed and settled for the night, Jessica and Jane sat down together to decide on a name.

"I should call her Jane, after you," she said. "No Jessica, not Jane, it is too plain. What about my second name which is Louise." Jessica liked the name Louise, so it was agreed. Jessica's second name was also Louise "I think I will shorten it to Lulu. I like the sound of that," announced Jessica. "I like that too," said Jane.

Life changed when Lulu came to live with Jane and Jessica. She was a beautiful big baby with soft fair skin and deep blue eyes. Her light-coloured hair would definitely be blonde as she got older.

Jessica loved being a mother. In fact, she thought it was the best thing she ever achieved so far in her life. She fed her until Lulu was three months old, when it was time for Jessica to resume her studies at the conservatorium of music. She decided to employ a nanny to assist whenever she was at university or rehearsals and used a breast pump to provide milk which was then frozen for her child.

Jessica and Jane interviewed six candidates for the position of a nanny for Lulu. The first one was an older woman with a severe looking face and an unpleasant manner. The second one was too young, only seventeen, and lacking in experience. Number three wanted to bring her two dogs. The dogs were very big. Number four was an unhealthy colour and was shabbily dressed. She did not look well. Number five was a man in his sixties. Number six was Emily Barry.

They discovered Emily was one of seven children and assisted her mother in the care of the younger ones. She was studying part time to be a childcare worker. Jane and Jessica, both liked her when she was interviewed. Emily was a confident young woman who loved babies.

Jessica was now required to do a lot more practical music with her violin, so on some evenings she needed to practice with other members of the university's orchestra. Emily was able to stay on those evenings. She was proving to be an excellent nanny, gentle and loving towards baby Lulu.

Chapter 26

Jessica was very busy with her studies and new baby, so further investigations into her birth were put on hold for the time being. She talked to Jane, and they decided to employ a private investigator to help in uncovering her adoption. "Well, it can't do any harm and I can afford it," said Jessica.

Jane knew of a man who did some investigative work for her in the past, so Jessica arranged to meet him at a nearby café. His name was Eric Marston and he began working as a private investigator over thirty years ago after retiring from the police force due to an injury on his back when he was attempting to chase down a burglar.

Eric seemed to be a kindly man who listened carefully to Jessica as she told him about her concerns. "It certainly does sound suspicious. Even more so, when there are no photographs or immunisation records. Did your mother have a habit of throwing out papers?" he asked. "No, actually it was the opposite. She was a bit of a hoarder," added Jessica.

Trinity Jessica Louise

Eric asked her if she kept anything else from her old home and she replied, "Not very much, but I will have a look. There are a few boxes of things at my storage unit".

They arranged a payment plan, and he told her he would get in touch after he completed a search of hospital births around the time of her suggested birth date and within a six-month period before and after. He asked her if she noticed any distinguishing marks on her body, "Why yes," Jessica said. "I have a small red birthmark about the size of a button on my right foot, and would you believe, my daughter Lulu has one in exactly the same spot," she added. "That might prove to be useful, "Eric said as he turned and left the café, leaving Jessica deep in thought. She never saw a birthmark on either of her parents. She was now absolutely certain she was adopted. Everything pointed to the undeniable fact.

Six weeks later, Jessica met once again with Eric Marston, her private investigator. Unfortunately, there was no good news. "I am really sorry Jessica, but I could find no births in any hospitals to match your own birth around the time we decided on. Of course, your biological mother may have decided to have a home birth if she was planning to give you away," he added. "What about the hospital at Springfield, the town nearest to Brinkley?" asked Jessica. "Yes, I thought of it and asked, however all of their records from twenty-one years ago were destroyed in a fire and no-one there could tell me anything," he replied.

They agreed to halt the investigation until further evidence could be found.

"I think I must put my search on hold," said Jessica to Jane at dinner the following night. "I do not think you need to give up just yet Jesssica. I think you should keep looking," Jane replied seriously.

Jessica was so busy with Lulu and her studies until term break halfway through the year. Lulu was nearly six months now and sleeping through the night. She was a beautiful baby, the image of her mother with her blue eyes and pretty golden curls. Jessica could also see some signs of James in her, especially his lovely smile.

Chapter 27

One evening when she was waiting for Lulu to wake up for her feed, Jessica remembered the boxes of items which she brought over from the storage unit. She started to go through them. They were mostly old newspaper cuttings of recipes, mixed in with a few old tea towels and used medicine bottles. One thing did catch her eye. It was a very faded child's toy, a fake fur blue rabbit. Jessica could barely remember the rabbit, but something told her it was hers. It seemed very familiar.

She opened the other box, which was similar in size, and inside with other rubbish she found a tiny silver rattle with a well-worn pink ribbon attached. She did not have any memory of the rattle. Underneath the rattle there were some numbers and letters engraved. She also found at the bottom of the box a very faded pink jumpsuit, probably one which would fit her daughter or someone around six to nine months. She wondered why it was there by itself with no other baby clothes. It must have been beautiful in its day, Jessica thought.

Jessica decided to contact Eric again. He met her at the same café, and she showed him what she found in the boxes. He said he would look into the make and model of the three items, if it was possible after so many years.

Eric asked Jessica if he could take the items, but for some reason she felt uncomfortable handing them over, so suggested to Eric that he photograph them instead. Eric did not like the idea but decided not to make a fuss since, she was paying him a lot of money and he wanted to remain on the job. He needed her to continue to hire him.

Eric was a nice man, but always short of cash. His new client Jessica Bloom seemed to have plenty of money, so he did not hesitate in attempting to draw out her case for as long as he could.

Eric visited a few country hospitals near Brinkley where Jessica was from. The Brinkley hospital was a small cottage hospital and could not find any records of a girl baby being born around the time of Jessica's birth. Eric decided to move on to the next town, namely Springfield.

When Eric approached the Springfield hospital, he was informed that even though a huge fire took place years go with most records lost, the town's local doctor could probably have helped him since he delivered all of the babies born in Springfield around twenty-one or twenty-two years ago.

Eric decided to keep the new piece of information to himself in order to prolong the case. After all, he told

Trinity Jessica Louise

himself, what were another few months, as the girl waited for years now to find her biological parents. He hoped the doctor would not die in the meantime. He did intend to talk to the doctor at some stage, but not just yet.

Chapter 28

Jessica was working hard with rehearsals with the Sydney symphony orchestra where she was enjoying playing the violin for the past few weeks. She absolutely loved playing in the orchestra and with the other members who were all keen musicians like herself. The orchestra was preparing for a huge concert at the Sydney Opera House where a famous international violinist would be playing his violin in three solo performances. Jessica was thrilled to be included in the orchestra. Jane loved hearing her practice each day.

In between feeding Lulu and rehearsals, Jessica was very busy. She still cooked every night for herself and Jane. She did not have time to continue her search for her biological parents then, hoping Eric was in control of everything, and would call if he found any information.

The first night of the concert arrived. Jane was attending the event, while Emily looked after Lulu who was now sleeping through the night.

When she arrived at the theatre, Jessica was told she was needed in the main office immediately. She was worried there might be something wrong. She thought perhaps she might not be able to play with the orchestra for some reason. She felt very anxious.

When she got to the office, she was informed of a serious car accident which involved the international violinist on the way from the airport, meaning he was not available to play. Now Jessica was required to perform the three violin solos. "But I can't. I am not ready, "she said nervously. "Yes, you definitely are more than ready, Jessica," replied the conductor. "I watched and listened to you over the past few months, and you are enormously talented. I have no doubt in my mind you can do this and will do it extremely well," he added with a smile.

Jessica was both amazed and confused as she prepared herself for the biggest moment in her life as a musician. She was a tiny bit nervous but overcame it as she stepped out for her performance. She knew that this was the opportunity of a lifetime and her dream come true.

She stepped out into the light, her blonde curls swirling around her shoulders and her blue eyes shining brightly. Her beautiful black dress, bought especially for the occasion, shimmered in the light.

This was the moment she always dreamed about since she was a child. Her only regret was the death of her parents, Jess and Will meant they could not there to see her. She thought they may have been watching on from heaven. Also, not there, was her first and only love, the father of little Lulu.

Jessica was given a standing ovation. She appeared three times to take a bow in front of an enthusiastic audience.

Her first solo performances were truly magnificent.

Chapter 29

Jessica started to make up her own compositions for the violin. She consulted her lecturers with what she compiled so far, and with their encouragement and advise, she could now play her own tunes on the violin. It was slow work at first, however Jessica was determined to complete at least two compositions before her next recital.

The first composition she called "Lullaby for Lulu. It was a gentle melody, well suited for children. It was a soft, soothing piece. The second composition was different because of its strong vibrant sound. She called it "Dream of Love" thinking of her love for James.

The two new compositions were approved for the next concert much to her delight.

Jane took Jessica shopping for an appropriate gown for her to wear at the next concert. After trying on a number of gowns, they both loved a deep navy dress with a heart shaped neckline and a full skirt which swirled around her ankles.

Chapter 30

Back in Springfield, Thomas and April were still very much in love, even after many years of marriage. Their loss of baby Trinity brought them closer rather than moving them apart. Thomas started planning something nice for their next wedding anniversary. He thought of having a party, but discounted the idea because he knew April would insist on helping with it, even if it was catered for. He wanted to do something different this year, something just for her, where she did not have to work.

Thomas heard about a huge concert coming to Sydney at the Opera House with a famous violinist performing and decided it would be just the thing he wanted. He obtained tickets at a very high price, not minding the cost and booked a night at one of Sydney's top hotels.

Thomas told April that they were taking a trip to Sydney, but not where they were going. He told her to bring her most beautiful gown, something special, was how he put it.

April decided to go to her favourite boutique in town to purchase "something special". She arrived home with a beautiful salmon pink gown and wrap, with shoes to match, packing it in her suitcase along with the lovely diamond necklace which Thomas gave her when Trinity was born all of those years ago.

They left for Sydney one beautiful sunny day and arrived in the afternoon at the hotel. Thomas previously booked into a famous restaurant for an early dinner. April looked charming in her new gown with her blonde curls round her shoulders and her blue eyes sparkling. "This is a wonderful treat," she said. "It's not over yet," Thomas replied. April was still a beautiful woman and in spite of the loss of their daughter did not seem to have aged very much at all.

They took a taxi from the restaurant to the Opera house. April's eyes lit up when they arrived at the concert hall and were escorted to their seats.

They did not have to wait too long before the curtain went up.

The concert master came to the front of the stage and informed the attendees of the accident to the international violist, and tonight his place would be taken by the orchestra's newest and most brilliant member of the orchestra, Miss Jessica Bloom.

Jessica started to play, enthralling the audience from the very first moment.

April and Thomas watched the beautiful girl on the stage. April whispered to Thomas "I know that girl."

Interval came, giving April and Thomas time to talk. "How can you possibly know the violinist?" he asked his wife. "I don't know," she replied. "There is something about her I recognise," she added. "You know April, she looks exactly like you, when you were her age," he said softly. "Perhaps she is a long lost relative," he suggested.

Jessica was given a standing ovation.

Thomas asked if he could take his wife backstage after the stunning performance Jessica gave. He wanted to meet this mystery girl.

April recognised a friend in the orchestra who introduced them to Jessica. "That was a brilliant performance," said April. "Thank you," replied Jessica. It was like a dream come true for me."

"Have you been playing long?" asked April, curiously. "Yes, since I was five years old. My mother initially taught me to play the violin and the piano, and then my parents found me a wonderful violin teacher," replied Jessica. "How amazing. She must be very proud of you," said Thomas. "She would be, but my parents are both dead," replied Jessica. April expressed her sorrow.

"You remind me of some-one," said Thomas. "Well, I don't have any relatives other than a first cousin of my mother's," said Jessica pleasantly, excusing herself to speak to another couple.

Thomas and April returned to their hotel, both curious about the lovely young violinist. They both felt as if they must have met her before, or at least may have known her parents when they were alive.

The next day they drove home to their property, still thinking about the beautiful girl whom they met the night before.

Chapter 31

Following her brilliant debut as a solo violinist, Jessica continued with her practice and studies. Jane was very proud of her, having thoroughly enjoyed her performance as well as listening to her daily practice. Lulu loved her mother playing to her and singing the sweet lullabies which she remembered hearing as a child from her own mother, Jess all those years ago. Jane adored Lulu. She was so glad she decided to take Jessica into her home all those months ago. It was almost as if Lulu was her own lost baby and Jessica was like her own daughter.

Baby Lulu was growing fast, now sitting up by herself and laughing and smiling a lot. She was a very happy little girl. Jessica loved taking her out in her pram because she interacted so well with people during their long walks. There was just something about her which caused people to stop and chat.

Jessica heard nothing from Eric, the private investigator for some time so decided to phone him for an update. He told her he was busy with other cases, which was quite untrue since he only took a few clients

Trinity Jessica Louise

at a time. He said he would get back on her case shortly, but he still remembered about her rattle and the little blue scruffy faded rabbit.

Jessic thought that perhaps he was really busy, but she was paying him good money and so far, there was not much to show from his investigations into the search for her biological family.

One day Roslyn Myer, her mother's cousin phoned her to say that she was going to the country in NSW to the small town of Brinkley where Jess and Will once live with Jessica. It seemed Roslyn's best friend Jean Bayfield and her husband Steven recently retired to the little town, six months ago and invited Roslyn to visit them there.

"I have never been there, so I am really looking forward to seeing the town where you grew up and the house you lived in," said Roslyn. "I thought you may have visited my family there in all the time we lived there," replied Jessica. "Well, I would have loved to have met you, but I was never invited, I don't know why," said Roslyn. "Yes, it does seem strange since you were my mum's only living relative and it was a big house with plenty of room," said Jessica thoughtfully. Roslyn said she would contact Jessica on her return and let her know how her former home was looking.

When she finished the phone call, Jessica started to think about her parents and wondered why they never invited Roslyn to visit. She also wondered why her parents never had any friends to visit, or why she was never allowed to have school friends stay overnight like other children did. At the time she didn't think about it too much because she rode her pony Tilly each day and played the violin and piano, so there was not much time to socialise. Whenever she asked to stay overnight with a friend, her parents always refused. They never gave her a reason.

The more she thought about it, the more she became worried. Even if she was adopted, there would have been no reason to avoid company. Why were her parents so secretive, Jessica wondered. While Jessica enjoyed plenty of occupations to keep her busy, her parents could still have invited friends or neighbours to visit and communicate with. She knew her parents guarded their privacy fiercely, but surely, they would have wanted to go to visit other people, go to barbeques and weekends away with friends like other families did.

Chapter 32

Roslyn set off for her visit to Brinkley in order to stay with her two old friends, Jean and Steven Bayfield. She travelled by train, enjoying the lovely view from the train window. Her friends met her at Brinkley station, and they drove the short distance to the Bayfield home. The Bayfield's purchased a few acres near the river which was surrounded by many tall gum trees. It was a beautiful house with a delightful garden full of fruit trees and seasonal shrubs.

"Will you take me to look at the house where the Blooms used to live when you have some free time," asked Roslyn one day. "Sure, not a problem, I would love to," replied Jean.

The next day was bright and sunny, so they took off towards the opposite end of town and around twenty minutes later arrived at the farm where Jessica grew up. The couple who leased the farm spotted the two ladies at the gate and invited them in, when they realised who they were. The two ladies enjoyed afternoon tea with the family.

Roslyn was pleasantly surprised at the beauty of the homestead and the surrounding gardens. She now understood why her cousin never wanted to leave such a lovely place and felt glad Jessica did not want to sell the place. She could now happily relate to Jessica on her return, about her former home being in good hands.

One evening Jean invited two new friends, a retired couple, Peter and Wendy Mills, for dinner. Roslyn helped with the meal preparation by making a pavlova for dessert.

The couple arrived and were introduced to Roslyn. During dinner Jean mentioned Roslyn was a cousin to Jess Bloom who lived in the town prior to her death.

"I remember Jess and Will," said Wendy. "Their deaths were such a terrible tragedy," she added. "Did you know Jessica, their daughter," asked Roslyn. "Yes, but only a little. I will never forget the day I first saw her," said Wendy. "She was about twelve months old, and Jess was holding onto her very tightly. I tried to find out where they adopted her from, but Jess immediately shut down and left the shop abruptly. It was very odd, because the baby just seemed to appear from nowhere. No-one knew where the baby came from or from which town or agency she was adopted. It was a bit of a mystery at the time. After that we rarely saw the baby. Will would mostly come to town to do the shopping alone, but neither Jess nor Will ever brought the baby. It was almost like they were trying to hide her," she added.

"Yes, I did not know anything about the baby until she was about two years old. And then I only heard about

Trinity Jessica Louise

the child on the grapevine. Jess never told me. Jess never told me anything about her pregnancy or the birth of her child and I never met Jessica until the day of the funeral," said Roslyn thoughtfully.

She resolved to phone Jessica when she got home to update her with the story Wendy had told her.

When Roslyn returned home, she telephoned Jessica to update her on what she knew about her as a baby. "It almost sounded to me like you were not adopted, but rather you could have been abducted," announced Roslyn to a shocked Jessica. "Why do you think that" answered Jessica, now very upset. "The secrecy has me worried. If you were adopted, why were your parents so secretive and why did they keep you hidden. When people adopt a child, usually it is a time of rejoicing. It just doesn't add up," added Roslyn. "They kept you hidden on the farm, only letting you go to pony club and church. They also home schooled you." she said seriously.

"But I wanted to home schooled," replied Jessica. "Even so, I am sure they were happy to allow you to be schooled at home," said Roslyn. "Yes, they were," said Jessica. "Did you ever go to town with them? asked Roslyn. "No, I never went to town. When I went to High school I went on the bus, straight there and straight back," Jessica added. "They never allowed me to go shopping in town like my friends did," said Jessica thoughtfully.

When Jessica pondered on what Roslyn said to her on the telephone, things all of sudden seemed to make sense at last. Her parents' strange behaviour when she was a baby, the lack of photographs, the toy rabbit and jumpsuit plus the silver rattle. Jessica then thought what Roslyn believed might just be true.

As incredible as it seemed to be, Jessica now realised it was possible she may have been the victim of an abduction. The only thing she could not understand was why her parents abducted her, and where did they get her from. Was she just taken her from a hospital or from a pram and if so, why was there no mention of it anywhere, she wondered. Now that her parents were dead, she might never know the truth.

Chapter 33

Back home at Springfield, April and Thomas returned to their busy lives. They still talked about their wonderful anniversary night in Sydney at the opera house and their meeting with the most extraordinary violinist, Jessica Bloom.

"You know, Thomas, I really felt as if I knew Jessica Bloom somewhere before, but I can't for the life of me think where it was," April announced one evening when they were having coffee and port after dinner, one of the few times during their busy days when they could have a conversation of any significance. "Yes, I can't get Jessica out of my mind either. She is so beautiful. She reminds me so much of you when I first met you," he answered.

"Maybe I will look her up on google," said April. "That's a good idea," replied her husband.

April decided to see if the internet could give her any clues as to the girl's background.

She typed in Jessica Bloom and found several articles mentioning her music achievements. There was a small biography which stated that Jessica was brought up in a small country town in NSW. The article said her parents died in a car accident two years ago, and Jessica lived abroad, after their deaths, for a time in Europe and London. There was not much else in the article, leaving April to still wonder where or when she first met Jessica Bloom.

Several weeks passed and then April discovered Jessica Bloom was to give another violin performance at the Opera House with the Sydney Symphony Orchestra. This time she would be playing two of her new compositions. April asked Thomas if they could go. "Of course we must go, my dear, if only to see and hear the lovely girl again," he said.

They set off once more for Sydney, staying again at the same hotel. Thomas booked tickets for the performance.

Once seated, the performance began and again the audience was in raptures as Jessica played her own compositions on the violin.

Afterwards Thomas and April went backstage to meet Jessica. This time she was accompanied by an older woman whose name was Jane.

"Congratulations my dear on your two lovely compositions. They were both very moving," said April enthusiastically. "I especially loved the Lullaby for Lulu," she added.

Jessica introduced Jane as her good friend with whom she lived. "Have you always lived in Sydney? April asked,

"No, I grew up in a small country town called Brinkley. You have probably never heard of it," she answered.

April was stunned. "Did you say Brinkley?" asked April. "We live in the next town of Springfield," replied Thomas. "Oh, I know that town. We used to go through it when I went to my violin lessons with a private teacher every Saturday, morning," said Jessica. "Did you go to school in Brinkley," asked April. "Yes, I was dux of the high school one year. You may have seen my photograph in the local paper," she added.

"Perhaps if you ever go to your hometown for a visit, you might like to visit us at our property which is just outside of Springfield," April said. "I would enjoy visiting your property very much thank you," replied Jessica.

Later April said to Thomas "That's where I knew her from, the photograph in the local newspaper." "Maybe, but she still seems very familiar," replied Thomas thoughtfully. "There is just something about the girl which makes me think I have known her before. You know April, she reminds me of you years ago when we first met at university," added Thomas.

Chapter 34

Jessica started to think about her private investigator. "I don't think he is trying very hard," she said to Jane one day. "Why don't you tackle it by yourself and forget about him," Jane replied. "Good idea," said Jessica who was sick of waiting for answers from the investigator.

"I really think I may have been abducted locally, around the Brinkley area, or somewhere close to the town, so I will start there," Jessica added.

Jessica decided to take a trip to Brinkley to see if she could find out the origin of either the blue rabbit or the silver rattle. She left Lulu with Emily who was happy to have the extra babysitting money. Of course, Jane was there to assist Emily when needed.

Jessica decided to travel to Brinkley in her own little car which she bought just a few months ago. It was a small Japanese car, just perfect for her, Jane and Lulu. She drove straight to Brinkley and booked into the only motel in town, called "The Midtown". It was a few years since she was last in the town, but nothing was very different. The shops all looked the same and a few new homes sprung up in the outer parts of the town, housing people from the city who were looking for a lifestyle change.

Jessica took a short detour to look at her old home. The couple were thrilled to see her and showed her all of their experimental crops and new ideas. Jessica was pleased they were keeping the farm in such good condition for her parents' sake.

After she checked into the motel room, Jessica made her way to the shops in the main street. She went first to a baby shop to ask about the blue rabbit, but the owners said that they never stocked an item such as the toy rabbit. The assistant at the Jewellery store was young. She phoned her boss, the owner of the store to ask about the rattle. He said he never stocked baby rattles, but he knew the Jewellery store in nearby Springfield might stock baby rattles, or they used to years ago.

The following day, Jessica made her way to Springfield, the next town. There was no luck with the rabbit, but the jeweller was more helpful. "Did you stock this type of rattle around twenty years ago?" asked Jessica. "Well, yes, we did," replied Mr. Adams, the jeweller. I have no idea who would have purchased such a rattle. They are pure silver, so quite expensive."

"My wife might have some idea, who may have purchased such an item. Clearly, they would have been wealthy with a lot of money to spend. My wife is away visiting her sick mother. I am not sure when she will return, but I will take a photograph of the rattle and ask her about it when she returns. I will also take down your telephone number," he said, helpfully.

Chapter 35

Returning to the Springfield Police station, Constable Jennings found a woman waiting to see him. Her name was Edith Jones, and she was the mother of Billy Jones

"What can I do for you Mrs. Jones?" asked Constable Jennings politely. "Well, I am missing a lot of my prescribed medications," she said. "What do you mean by missing, Mrs. Jones?" asked Constable Jennings. "Well, I take tablets to help me, when I am feeling a bit down," said Mrs. Jones. "Lately I have been noticing that some of my tablets are missing from the packs. I take Prozac and Mirtazapine. I have been taking them for years," she said. "Have any gone missing at any other time?" asked Constable Jennings.

"Yes, over the years a lot have gone missing. I counted out about fifteen tablets missing one time. Another time I was missing ten and yet another time, I seemed to misplace twelve. I know that I am not a well person, but I am very good at taking my pills, always have been, so I know when there are some missing," she added. "Could your husband have taken them?" asked Constable

Jennings. "No, he doesn't believe in taking pills," she added.

"What about your son. Would he have taken any of them?" asked Constable Jennings. "Well, yes, perhaps he could have. He is usually in some kind of trouble, and I think he might have taken them to sell, as he is always short of money. I don't want to accuse him, but I don't want to think he may be selling them to school children either. They are extremely powerful drugs," she added.

"You have done well to come to us Mrs. Jones. Is it possible for you to bring in any of the packets of the tablets so that we know what we are dealing with here?" he asked. "Yes, I don't throw the packets out very often. I am a bit of a hoarder. I don't know why I still have all of these empty boxes in my closet" She replied.

Two days later Mrs. Jones returned to the police station with two plastic bags full of empty tablet packets, leaving them at the station for Constable Jennings.

Constable Jennings took the packets to the local pharmacist to see if the two tablets found at Mavis Beatty's place of death could match any of the packets. They were in luck. The two tablets came from two of the empty packets.

Constable Jennings could hardly believe it. He now had the evidence to get a conviction for the death of Mavis Beatty. Jimmy and Billy were already in gaol. The new findings would mean that the two of them would never be released. No-one would care, but justice would be served for poor Mavis who did not deserve to be murdered at such a young age.

Chapter 36

Jessica returned home feeling hopeful. She thought at last she was starting to get somewhere in her search for her biological parents. She now believed it was extremely likely that she may have been abducted as a baby and was feeling positive about the Jeweller's wife being able to identify the little silver rattle.

About two weeks later she received a phone call from the jeweller in Springfield. His wife was home and wanted to see the rattle itself in order to make a proper identification.

Jessica decided to return to Springfield, taking baby Lulu with her this time. She packed her car with all of Lulu's baby needs and set off early in the morning.

Lulu behaved very well on the trip, sleeping in her carry cot or sitting in her car seat. Before she left, Jessica telephoned April and Thomas to let them know she would be coming to Springfield. "Of course, you must stay with us," said April with enthusiasm. "There is just one thing I need to tell you first," added Jessica. "I do have a child with me," she said. "That will be fine. We love children," replied April.

When April arrived at Springfield, she stopped in the town to see the jeweller's wife. The woman looked at the rattle and said "Yes it was one of ours. We stocked them over twenty years ago. They are not as popular today. "Do you recall who may have purchased it?" asked April, hopefully. "I think it could have been one of two ladies, both wealthy. One was Mrs. Roberts, but she has passed away now, and I think the other woman may have been Mrs. Langley senior. She used to live at Langley Park but now she lives in town with her husband," said Mrs. Adams.

"How strange. I am going to stay at a place called Langley Park tonight," she added. "Well, that will be with April and Thomas Langley. Mrs. Langley is Thomas's mother," she added.

Jessica decided to find Mrs. Langley the next day. By now it was getting late and little Lulu was starting to get hungry. Her search was nearly over, but she could wait one more day.

Jessica drove the few short kilometres to Langley Park. She admired the beautiful trees lining the road into the property. In front of her was the delightful old homestead, painted white, with verandas all around. It was surrounded by magnificent gardens, full of rose bushes and many native shrubs.

Jessica stepped out of the car and lifted baby Lulu from her car seat. Lulu was dressed in a lovely floral dress. She heard footsteps coming from inside the house.

Trinity Jessica Louise

Suddenly she recognised April and her tall handsome husband, Thomas standing at the front door to greet her.

April walked to Jessica's car and looked at the baby, now in her mother's arms. "Oh my God," she exclaimed. "What is it, my dear?" asked Thomas looking worried. "Come and look at the baby," she said to Thomas.

"What is wrong?" asked Jessica, feeling a bit alarmed. "Oh, it's nothing. It's just that your baby is so beautiful," replied April, attempting to cover up her shock when she saw the baby. "How old is she?" asked Thomas. "Well, she is now nine months old," replied Jessica. "Her name is Louise, but we call her Lulu," she added.

Thomas looked at his wife. They were both thinking exactly the same thing. They were both stunned when they looked at baby Lulu.

"Lulu looks exactly like you Jessica," said April, as she gazed lovingly at the beautiful baby. "Yes, I believe she does. Everyone has told me the same thing from the moment she was born," said Jessica.

"Well, come inside Jessica and Lulu," said Thomas, remembering his manners, after the shock he just received.

"What will you have to drink?" asked Thomas as they were all seated outside on the veranda. "Sparkling water would be great. Do you mind if I feed Lulu some supper?" asked Jessica "Not at all," replied April, nervously.

"Would you like to hold Lulu?" asked Jessica. "Oh, my goodness, yes please," replied April, excitedly. As April held the baby girl, the memories came flooding back to twenty-two years ago. Thomas looked on with tears in his eyes.

Jessica fed her daughter some canned custard and then decided to change her nappy. "May I come with you?" asked April as she took Jessica to the guest bedroom which she prepared for her stay.

Jesssica removed Lulu's nappy and gently washed her little body with a facecloth, before putting some baby powder on her. Lulu giggled softly.

"What is that red mark on her foot?" asked April. "Oh that, well it's a birthmark. I have one too, in exactly the same place," replied Jessica as she lifted her jeans up to show April.

"Jessica, were you adopted?" April asked softly. "Yes, probably. I know that Jess Bloom was not my biological mother because I have done the DNA testing, but there seems to be some mystery around my birth. I think I may have been abducted when I was a baby." she added. "Why do you think that, Jessica?" asked April. "Well for a start, my birth certificate was forged, there are no photographs of me as a baby or growing up, and my parents kept me hidden and rarely took me out to town or to places where I might have been seen. I was home schooled as well until high school when my parents never attended any functions or events," Jessica added. "I have been searching for my biological parents for years now since Jess and Will Bloom were killed," she said.

Trinity Jessica Louise

Thomas entered the room then. He heard what Jessica told April. "Jessica, we had a baby girl once, about twenty-two years ago. She was abducted from our car during a rodeo, and we have never been able to find her. We have been searching for her for more than twenty years," said Thomas.

Just then April lifted up her skirt and showed Jessica the red birth mark on her foot. It was exactly the same as the birth mark on both Jessica and Lulu.

Jessica went to her suitcase and took out the silver rattle, the little blue rabbit, and the faded pink jumpsuit and handed them to April, her mother.

EPILOGUE

The next day Constable Jennings paid a visit to the Langley family.

Following his latest interrogation of Jimmy and Billy, they at last remembered where they dropped off baby Trinity, on the night of the rodeo, over twenty-two years ago.

It was at a farmhouse traced to Jess and Will Bloom, just outside Brinkley. There they lived, and raised their daughter Jessica, for almost nineteen years, until they were killed in a car accident near their home.

AUTHORS NOTE

My special thanks to friends in Bacchus Marsh and Deniliquin, also my soul food friends for their continued support and encouragement.

Soul food in Bacchus Marsh is a very special place where guests come every week for a home cooked meal, bread, dessert, fruit and other goods when things are tough or lonely. Around 20 volunteers cook over 120 meals each week.

All of us, young or old, need to be loved, fed, respected and cared for.

My special thanks to my daughters Lara and Emily and granddaughters Ruby, Chloe and Amalia for their support in everything I do.

www.ingramcontent.com/pod-product-compliance
Lightning Source LLC
LaVergne TN
LVHW040146080526
838202LV00042B/3040